The Barefoot Nuns of Barcelona
& other short stories...

A collection of stories from the
Orange Northern Woman Short Story Prize

GREER PUBLICATIONS LTD

First published in Great Britain in November 2005 by Greer Publications Ltd

Copyright @ Greer Publications Ltd 2005

ISBN 0-9551824-0-9

Cover illustration by
Helen Wright

Designed and produced by
The Magazine Centre
www.themagazinecentre.com

Printed by
W & G Baird Ltd

Greer Publications Ltd
5b Edgewater Business Park
Belfast Harbour Estate
Belfast, BT3 9JQ
Northern Ireland

www.greerpublications.com

Foreword

Orange is passionate about literature. And we're very proud to be celebrating the fifth year of the Orange Northern Woman Short Story Prize, with the publication of this collection of short-listed stories from each year of the competition.

It reflects our support for a whole range of literary projects, from the Orange Prize for Fiction – now celebrating its tenth birthday and recognised as one of the UK's most powerful and prestigious awards – to *Chatterbooks*, which runs reading groups for children in libraries across the UK.

The great thing about the Orange Northern Woman Prize is that it gives budding writers the chance to develop their skills and it has inspired women who have never written a story before to give it a go. And that's exactly what the Prize was set up to do: to help nurture and encourage new writing talent.

I'd like to thank everyone at Northern Woman for all their hard work on the Prize over the past five years – particularly Lyn Palmer and Mary Carson. Thanks also go to our celebrity literary judges, like Sheila O'Flanagan and Glenn Patterson, who have given the Prize real stature.

To all the authors published here, and to the hundreds of authors who have entered the competition over the years, on behalf of Orange, I wish them all a bright future.

Jonathan Rose
Head of Community Affairs
Orange UK

Introduction

In the minds of many people, the short story is a unique and incandescent creature. Ever-changing, it can shock, surprise, thrill and move. It will demand complete absorption from the reader, whilst leaving them ever wanting more. For this very reason, some readers love the short story; and for the same reason, others dislike it with a passion. What is indisputable, however, is that the short story favours the brave – writers willing to step off the edge of the precipice and take a risk.

And it was with these very adventurers in mind that the Orange Northern Woman Short Story Prize was conceived. Since 2001, Northern Woman Magazine has joined forces with Orange to host the Short Story Prize – an event which has developed into an annual landmark in Northern Ireland's literary calendar.

In hosting the Prize, we consider ourselves very fortunate to have found such committed partners in Orange; and our sincere thanks must go to Orange UK Head of Community Affairs, Jonathan Rose, for his unstinting help and support.

At the heart of this competition lies a deep commitment to the nurturing of local female literary talent, and to the encouragement of self-expression. Each year, it has become harder and harder to whittle down the torrent of entries to a brief short-list of finalists. In this endeavour, I have been immensely grateful for the continued insight and expertise of award-winning Irish authors Sheila O'Flanagan and Glenn Patterson. The element of surprise, an unusual twist, and intriguing finale and true-to-life characters – all have played their part in our annual selection process.

Ultimately, though, what has set apart the successful entries collected in this anthology is that each author has submitted a story we know our readers will appreciate and identify with; and every story is as unique as the women who have penned them.

I hope you enjoy dipping into this collection as much as I know our authors have enjoyed their part in the process. Perhaps it will even inspire some of you to pick up a pen, take a risk, and create something special of your own.

Lyn Palmer
Editor
Northern Woman magazine

2001

WINNER

BABY
by Anjali Sachdeva

FINALISTS

CHANGING REFLECTIONS
by Teresa Davey

CROWNING GLORY
by Lindsay Hodges

INTO THE FAR UNKNOWN
by Elizabeth Kennedy

MY DAUGHTER, OH MY DUCATS!
by Geraldine Burke

THE AUL WAN
by Lily McWilliams

THE COMEDOWN QUEEN
by Mary Fitzgerald

THE SADDEST WOMAN I HAVE EVER KNOWN
by Shannon McLaughlin

2002

WINNER

CARNIVAL
by Sonia Haddad

FINALISTS

PROPER PEOPLE
by Lily McWilliams

RELIEF
by Jennifer Hampton

REVELATIONS
by Rosie Akeroyd

SILENT CALL
by Teresa Davey

SWAN LAKE
by Heather Richardson

THE COAST ROAD
by Mary-Clare Smith

THE DAY HE LEFT
by Julie Harte

2003

WINNER

LONG ANNA RIVER
by Rachael Kelly

FINALISTS

ANGEL
by Lesley Richardson

THE BAREFOOT NUNS OF BARCELONA
by Michelle Gallen

LOVE ALWAYS
by Carmel McQuaid

MAY BE
by Alison Bradley

A PHILOSOPHY OF LOVE
by JS Ferguson

2004

WINNER

THE SOFA MAN
by Bernadette Owens

FINALISTS

EPISTLE
by Bernie McGill

HALF A BROTHER
by Korenna Bailie

LIFE DRAWING
by Susan Gordon

TRAVELLERS
by Julie Agnew

TRESPASSING
by Michelle Gallen

WHAT COMES AROUND
by Pat Griffin

2005

WINNER

DOMESTIC EDUCATION
by Michelle Gallen

FINALISTS

A STILL LIFE
by Bernie McGill

BETTY/ELIZABETH
by Pauline McNulty

BITING THE BULLET
by Aideen D'Arcy

THE CALLING
by Katherine Caulfield

WORDS OF WISDOM
by Tammy Moore

Baby

by Anjali Sachdeva

The baby lived in a jar on the mantel. It was a bananas and peaches jar, because that was his favourite food, and it was inside a small gold box to make it more attractive. Two years ago he had been burnt into ashes, barely a handful because he was, after all, only a baby. But this seemed to make other people think that it was acceptable to have him sitting there. If she had kept him whole they would have had her put away somewhere in a jar of her own.

The first thing she had done after setting him up there was to move the couch so it faced the fireplace, instead of the television. She liked to sit and look at him, but she realised that there was really no telling what they had given her. They could be the ashes of a squirrel, or a bird, or a bundle of newspapers. Except that those would not talk to her in a baby's voice, or at least they would not be so convincing if they did.

She was in her room sitting at the mirror when she heard Dana's car pull up. The mirror showed her that her skin was pale, and the veins showed through in places. Bright red streaks in her hair where she had tried to dye the grey ones made her look whiter still. Dana rang the bell twice, knocked, and finally let herself in.

"Down in a minute, make yourself at home," Sarah called. She rubbed the tip of her index finger first into an oval compact of eye shadow, then onto her eyelid. She could feel the bulb of her eye rolling beneath the closed lid like a seed of flesh implanted in her face. When her make-up was complete she went downstairs.

Dana had refrained, for once, from looking through her cupboards, and was sprawled on the couch reading a magazine. She wore a short, green skirt and a shrunken sweater that she had fished off her floor that morning. Her lipstick was the same bright pink she had chosen in secondary school. When she glanced up from the magazine and saw Sarah's face she let out a shriek of indignation and sprang off the couch with a vitality Sarah found surreal.

"He didn't! What happened this time?"

"Nothing. Let's just go."

"It's not *nothing*. Last month there were those burns on your arm, and now a black eye, and next time who knows what! You should just divorce him. He's the worst thing that ever happened to you."

Sarah felt her throat tighten, but she softened her voice into supplication.

"I'll be all right. He's at the pub, and if we can leave before he gets back he won't know where I went. Please."

Her desperation won out over Dana's sense of moral outrage. Fifteen minutes later they were driving to the mall.

At the mall Dana linked her fingers through Sarah's as they walked. Sarah was treated to a manicure, and a new sundress, and a kiss on the cheek whenever she looked unhappy. When she dropped a vase in Debenham's the salesgirl patted her arm and told her not to worry about it. Sometimes people passing by pivoted their heads to catch a second glimpse of her battered face, and if she happened to meet their eyes they gave her a half-curious, half-sympathetic smile.

When Sarah and Dana had both tired of trying to be cheerful they went to do their grocery shopping. The woman in front of them in the queue had a little boy sitting in the front of her cart. Dana flipped through a tabloid and offered interesting titbits about the stars, to which Sarah only nodded in reply while she watched the boy.

He looked about three years old, with blonde hair that was getting too long and dark brown eyes. He swung his legs back and forth, crashing his trainers against the cart and taking obvious pleasure from it.

"Stop it," said his mother. She was a tall woman, not older than twenty-two, with her hair wound into a bun at the back of her head. The boy looked at her for a moment and then went back to banging his feet.

Three carts ahead an elderly woman was arguing with the cashier over how many bonus points she was supposed to get for her groceries. The mother looked at her watch and huffed. Eventually the little boy stopped kicking and grabbed a candy bar off a nearby rack. A few seconds later he dropped it. His mother puckered her lips into a knot, bent down and retrieved the candy bar, and shoved it violently back onto the rack. She put her face up against the little boy's.

"I said, Stop It," she repeated, a bit too loudly. "What's the matter with you?"

"Sorry!" said the boy, dropping his eyes. But as soon as she moved back around to the side of the cart to glare at the cashier, he began looking around again. When he glanced Sarah's way she smiled at him. He stared at her for a minute before smiling back bashfully.

By now the cashier had called in the manager, and he was going down the old woman's grocery receipt item by item. He ticked each product off with a red pen, saying, "Ten *points,* twenty *points,* three *points* . . ." while she shook her head unhappily. The boy was still watching Sarah. She gave him a mischievous grin, and stuck her tongue out at him. He responded with a stream of giggles and bounced up and down in his excitement, but this shook loose a bottle of soy sauce that his mother had squeezed in next to him. The bottle fell to the floor and shattered.

The mother spun around and barked, "Patrick!" She took the little boy's hand and smacked it. He burst into tears, and she was going to slap him again when Sarah grabbed her wrist.

"No, don't do that," she said, aghast.

"Let go of me!" shrieked the woman.

Sarah had not even realised how tightly she was gripping. The woman wrenched her arm free, and white, finger-shaped marks remained on her wrist.

"But you shouldn't hit him."

"What's it to do with you?" snapped the mother. "If you want to let your own children become spoilt then that's your business. Touch me again and I'll have the manager call the police."

Sarah looked around. The cashier, the manager, and the elderly lady were all staring at them open-mouthed. Dana was studying her shoes. Patrick had stopped crying and was gaping at her. Finally Dana put an arm around her and led her away, past the cash register, abandoning their cart of groceries in the middle of the queue. As they walked out the door she could hear Patrick's voice behind her.

"That lady had a big purple eye, like the monster in our storybook at home," he said to his mother. The woman's answering laughter beat against the inside of Sarah's head like marbles spilling onto a pane of glass.

Halfway home Dana decided to pretend that nothing had happened, and resumed her gossiping. When they finally reached the house Sarah persuaded her to leave by promising to phone right away if Colin got out of hand.

When Dana's voice faded away the house became quiet, and she could hear the baby again. He had always slept the whole night through, and had died soundlessly in his crib, but now he seemed to talk at all hours of the day and night. His small gurgles and long, keening vowels had evolved to the point where he could almost say her name.

"He didn't stay mad at his mommy for even a minute," she said pleadingly, sitting on the sofa. The baby only laughed.

At half seven she went upstairs to the bedroom. Dying summer light flooded through the windows. She sat down at the mirror again, opened a jar of cold cream and massaged it in tiny circles across her face. She rubbed harder around her eye, and then took a tissue from the box and began wiping the make-up away. Deep streaks of aubergine stained the tissue, and the hollow of her black eye grew pale to match the rest of her skin. When she had finished she examined herself in the mirror. Her face was now clean and symmetrical, the cosmetic bruise discarded with the tissue in the bin. She took the compact of purple eye shadow off the vanity table and put it in a drawer under her socks.

Colin came home at eight. His boots barely left the ground as he walked up the driveway, and the weight of a double shift at the factory hunched his shoulders. But when he saw her waiting in the doorway he smiled, and straightened up a bit. As he stepped inside he wrapped his arms around her waist kissed her.

"I don't know how I'd ever get through work if I didn't have you to come home to."

He shrugged off his heavy denim jacket and then stood in front of the sofa while she kneeled down to unlace his work boots for him.

"What's my darling been up to all day?" he asked, stroking her hair.

His hand felt impossibly heavy on her head, as though the weight of his touch might snap her neck.

"Just waiting for you."

He stepped out of the boots and pulled her gently down onto the couch, and kissed her throat. Her fingers clenched where they rested on the cushions. She could not turn her head enough to see the mantel, but inside his jar she heard the baby begin to cry.

Changing Reflections

by Teresa Davey

Gone were the days when a quick dab of lipstick was enough.

Now it was the most important job of her day, to make herself presentable to the world she inhabited, or for that matter any world that impinged on the one she had made her home in. She did not wish to let her guard down before any of them.

She didn't care about the workmen who may come within her range to take care of something that may have broken down, she didn't care about the shop assistants who barely looked at her, but still she had to put on the mask. The only person who was allowed to see the real Louise was Louise. All those people she called her friends were not allowed to see her as she really was, just as she never saw the real them. As she sat at the mirror she realised that this meant she was her only true friend, because true friends cherished the closeness that came with honesty.

Her circle were in essence children once more, girls wearing school uniforms that covered their different shapes and personalities, that said you must conform. Often the exuberance of youth meant that they fought to allow themselves expression. At this end of the equation, exuberance was gone and they were happy to take shelter behind conformity. These days, their uniform was defined by 'label', by this season's colour and style, and they had to be hung on the right shape of clotheshorse. All of this had to be accompanied by the regulation look of the image-conscious, confident, older woman. In other words they were the creation of others and so ended their lives as they had begun them so long ago, with their distinctive shape and personalities covered up.

Of all her friends she couldn't think of one whom she would want to reveal herself to. Occasionally a group of them would go away together but they never shared rooms. They needed their privacy. They needed their time alone. They were again all the same in not wanting others to see through their false reflections.

Even her two daughters had been relegated to a space beyond that which her real self inhabited. How had that happened, she asked herself? When had she begun to retreat from her own true image and allowed it to become buried? She couldn't really remember. Had it been a sudden moment or a gradual stepping back? No, much as she tried, she couldn't remember.

She thought the answer was hiding somewhere in that murky mesh of memory that revolved around the time when her two daughters had gone off to university and her husband was still working. Lost in time, she found refuge by focusing on her bodily, rather than her spiritual needs. She now realized that she had sacrificed herself on the altar of those who wished to feed on her. She had begun a round of being massaged, exercised, dieted, doctored, groomed, dressed and controlled. She had been made to feel that it was worthy to attend charitable coffee mornings and sit on committees. Her refuge had turned out to be a retreat from life.

She had not allowed herself to experience life, to discover her *raison d'être*. She had not allowed herself to put a few essentials on her back, boots on her feet, comfortable clothes on her body and set off to meet the world, breathing in its air and inspiration. How could she exist without all the trappings that had gradually imprisoned her so stealthily with their counterfeit caring? Later when her husband retired, he had gradually given up suggesting last-moment outings or wacky holiday ideas, as they would always clash with her endless round of activity.

She suddenly felt both weary and wise. She knew that she was filling in her time before she would follow her husband into the void. The deception of an idealised afterlife was just another thing to keep people, not just women, in order. She knew this now but what could she do? She felt as though she had already inhabited death's anteroom. She knew that the only other person destined to see the real her was the undertaker if she was lucky enough to die suddenly. Otherwise a couple of nameless nurses and a doctor might also be party to that dubious honour.

Was she slightly unstable now because of her husband's recent untimely death? Probably. Yet she could console herself with the thought that he had done so much. She felt guilty, that she had deprived their relationship of her attention. Her husband never criticised her, believing that she should have the freedom to live her life as she wished. At least she supposed that was what he believed. He had begun to go off alone. He had told her that while he would have liked her to join him he also enjoyed travelling alone, because he always met such interesting people. To console himself perhaps, he had said that when two people travel together they sometimes become too cosy and don't reach out to connect with other people.

Before he died he had told her that if he could have one wish for her it would be that she would 'live' her years yet to come. She had laughed and said she was happy, that she enjoyed herself in her own way, that not everyone wanted the same things in life. Now that he was dead she realised the truth. How could she be happy if she couldn't reveal her true self to another person, even if that was because she didn't know her true self? Could she now at this late stage grant her husband his last wish and live her life, not just fill her time? Was she strong enough to do that, she asked herself?

Louise sat on the plane and thought of her late husband. She felt a warmth surround her that was in some way connected with him. "Thank you Tom," she said softly. She had lived more in this past year than ever before, it seemed. She took out her small compact and lipstick and put on a dab while she looked at her reflection. Yes, she had a small birthmark on her cheek but so what – that was part of her. She looked healthily tanned if not slightly weather-beaten. Her hair was...well, it was OK... neat enough. It would do until she got home and the shade of grey it had become really wasn't bad with its natural highlights. She smiled as she looked down at her hands and the neatly clipped nails that now replaced their manicured predecessors.

She couldn't wait to see her daughters, the daughters she seemed to have rediscovered as people even though, geographically, she had been further away from them this past year than ever before. She, Louise, grandmother, widow and pillar of society, had bought herself a round the world air ticket as though she had been a young, carefree student. Not quite the student, true, for she had security and money in the bank.

Before she had departed, she asked her daughters to spend a little time with her while she cleared out the family home and then she had shocked them with her plans. Her daughters initially thought she was suffering from a grief reaction over their father's death, which, in a way, she was. But, for several days they talked, and talked, until they realised their mother was a person they could relate to in depth once more.

Later, they became excited about her plans, though they cautioned her to be careful. They followed her journey on a map put up on their walls at home as many parents do when their children take a year out. They looked forward to her letters telling of her experiences, photographs showing her metamorphosis into a confident and fulfilled person. They looked forward to her phone calls, e-mails and her return home. They vied over which daughter she would stay with first while she looked for an apartment that wouldn't take up much of her time.

They wondered what their mother was going to do next.

Crowning Glory

by Lindsay Hodges

Brooding at the back of an endless Post Office queue in Bedford Street, I couldn't take my eyes off the scalp of the man in front. His hair was cropped so close to the skin that only a distant memory of curl remained.

I gaped at this skull, fascinated by the five o'clock shadow that covered every undulation. Although little more than stubble protruded, the hairs still followed a pattern, an asymmetric fold of stunted follicles. The whorls conjured an image of a thumbprint, the black-inked evidence of a criminal investigation. If the customer proved to be an armed bank robber, I could select him from a police line-up from the back view alone. My fingers itched to touch his scalp, anticipating the sharp strike of a matchbox, followed by flaring temper.

Other people's hair had become something of an obsession since I lost my own, shaved to the bone after a car accident two years before. The regrowth fell like Icarus, never to reappear. Post traumatic shock, the medical examiner said. Under my baseball cap, I imitated Duncan Goodhew without the swimming ability. The scowl of a wine-dark scar disfigured my scalp from the base to the crown. Ridged from the imprint of staples, it still smouldered from the insult of surgery. My left temple dipped into a small hollow, a tender fontanelle paying tribute to the missing bone, which fragmented on impact with the windscreen. The resulting wound tattooed the University Boat Race to my forehead, a stencil of hand-stitched oars in perfect symmetry astride a scull stroked only by my son.

I've heard amputees confess that when a limb is severed, only crazed itch haunts the space where flesh and bone inhabited. My fingers, driven by memory alone, still reach up towards an absent fringe, sweeping imaginary strands from my face.

I have developed an empathy with men suffering premature alopecia, offering doe-eyed succour as they pass in supermarkets, tenacious wisps of hair still clinging to their brows. Though each heroic strand is combed with painstaking care over the unloved dome, the wind claims instant sacrifice outside the inner sanctum of the store.

My fanatical research uncovered only one man who didn't fit the profile of exfoliated disappointment. The fitness instructor at my local gym exposed his denuded cranium with pride, not through vanity or illness – somehow he looked as if he'd never grown hair. His skull shone in the health club mirrors, a glacier-scooped drumlin. I learn amateur phrenology as I tread the step machine with limping gait, assessing every bump and ridge as he pumps iron. Unlike the Post Office robber, this scalp speaks to me of intelligence and compassion. Perhaps he might understand my dilemma.

The only head I cannot bear to study is my own, concealing my inadvertent striptease under a parade of baseball caps, headscarves and woolly hats. I lacked the audacity to appear bald in public, even to shock. Reactions in hospital waiting rooms reflected my own self-loathing. Adults glanced away in embarrassment, while children shrank into comforting arms, sobbing.

A primeval fear of scar tissue snaking from the brain alarmed strangers, assuming a full frontal lobotomy. They whispered about my condition as if I was subhuman, the epitome of everything they dreaded most.

As the prospect of returning to work loomed closer, I accepted the need for a permanent remedy, but finding a comfortable disguise proved a challenge of matter over mind. My reflection revolted me as I tried one faux hairstyle after another, a circus clown in my local hairdresser's shop. Some of the wigs sprouted real curls, an unhappy prostitution of pliant hair for hard cash. Blonde, brunette, short or curly, my changing face and extending tresses mesmerised the regulars, but unsettled me to breaking point.

If I ever survived the slow torture of the Post Office queue, I had an appointment with the medical stylist. Having put off the ordeal three times already, my doctor had threatened to send me for psychiatric evaluation if I postponed again. I took no pleasure from my condition, but it would take more than hair to induce amnesia. Wedding photographs show my dusky hair shining, a glossy aubergine, as Ryan slipped an arm round my waist. Now my widowed scalp is naked without my husband and daughter, lost forever when our car somersaulted the embankment.

Protected by premonition and his grandmother's guardianship, my baby became my double during my recovery, both of us tucked up in bed, hairless and drooling. Now Joe sports thick, lustrous curls like his father, unflinching when I bend close to steal a mother's kiss. I seek comfort from the touch and smell of his hair, longing for my daughter's cherry ringlets.

The Post Office queue expired at last. Mr Fingerprint airmailed a birthday card to his father, exposing my cranial predictions as fraudulent. As he strode away, I wondered if my flawed judgement now revealed the fitness instructor to be a serial killer. Posting a parcel of toddler photographs to Ryan's mother, my appointment with destiny could not be postponed any longer. A Number 60 bus travels close enough to the surgery. Driving would be more practical, but my nerves lay shredded amidst the crumpled metal. Where possible, I prefer to walk. On top of my workouts in the gym, I've never been fitter, regaining some bloom to my cheeks after anaemic months in hospital. It's only on the inside that the scars have not healed, wounds raw and aching with the loss of more than my hair.

Unaware of my neurosis, Joe revelled in the excitement of the bus, every journey an adventure in public transport. He gurgled at the mere sight of red and white livery. Paying our fare, I sat facing the front, adjusting my San Francisco 49ers baseball cap, the jealous guardian of my slaphead secret. My son chose my headgear for the day, another gift from a travelling friend who couldn't think of anything else to give me. Joe curls his fingers into my fist, chuckling at the spectacle of two women stepping onto the bus just before it pulled away from the stop, jaw-deep in conversation. Choosing to gabble in front of me, their high-pitched tones bounced off the Perspex window. I didn't hear a word they said, staring at their coiffeur instead as if they only existed from the neck up. One bottle blonde, one permed brunette.

Neither provided me with inspiration. Even though I would be spared the compulsion to curl, tint and dye, blonde streaks would only contrast with my dark eyebrows. As for the brunette, the very sight of her perm made my eyes water, as the tight nest of curls wrenched her scalp, making my scar line throb in sympathy. The smell of hairspray was overpowering, threatening to engulf the bus in a biohazard capable of single-handed destruction of the ozone layer.

I pressed the bell three stops early, in need of fresh air and self-belief. What did it matter how I looked, or what synthetic creation adorned my head? It would make little difference to Joe, who would hurl whatever covering I chose across the room, a furred Frisbee mid-air. No one else mattered, no potential lover yearning to run his fingers through my hair only to find it self-destruct in his hands. The decision came down to a stark choice – select a wig or see a shrink.

Pushing open the surgery door, I found the stylist waiting for me at reception.

She smiled, tossing a burnished auburn mane as she extended her hand. "We meet at last," she said. "Please come in and take off your cap." Following her into the surgery, I complied, reaching to flick an annoying strand of hair from my eyes. I caught myself mid-swipe. "Sorry," I said. "Force of habit."

Retracting a floral sheet with a flourish, she revealed a selection of synthetic wigs in all shapes and sizes, a burial ground of ceremonial scalps. "Try any of these," she said. "Once you make your choice, it will all be much easier from here. Trust me – I know about these things." Massaging the base of her neck with dextrous fingers, she removed the sleek pelt to reveal a covering of downy fuzz underneath. "Cancer last August," she said. "C'est la vie."

Closing my eyes, my hand levitated over the inanimate creatures. "Eeny, meeny, miny, moe," I said, settling on the middle animal. The fibres were smooth to the touch, entwining my fingers. "This one will do."

"Good choice," the stylist said, adjusting the hairpiece with infinite patience. "This will suit you very well."

I opened my eyes, reborn as a redhead. The image of my daughter smiled back from the hand-mirror, approving, but my breath caught at the sight of Joe's anxious expression. I knelt in front of my son.

Knitting his eyebrows, he stared up at me, eyes huge with confusion. Then he reached stubby fingers towards my hair. "Mummy," he said. "Pretty."

Into the Far Unknown

by Elizabeth Kennedy

The yellow forsythia buds were bursting into springtime blossom and her father was dying.

Kathryn could feel a huge and overwhelming blanket of sobs smothering her as she crossed the hospital car park towards her car. She fumbled blindly with keys and set off the car alarm. It wailed around her as she choked for breath, vision blurred, and finally fell into the driver's seat. Beaten, she put her head against the cold steering wheel and howled in a way that she hadn't done since she was a child.

Four old men in a hospital ward, bodies clinging to life, minds long departed elsewhere. One wartime conscript was the most desperate of all, thinking that he had returned to a Japanese prisoner of war camp, constantly trying to escape; digging, digging, then bolting for freedom. At least her father's confusion was fairly absolute. It was less often now that he anxiously strove to put some order back into the world; mostly he was totally detached from all around him. He still shook his head fiercely though, as if to try and regain control over his muddled thoughts.

It was how he had shaken her that sunny day when she was six or less; she'd been soaring skywards on the swing, almost drunk with giddiness. He'd arrived home from work early in the afternoon and told her off for going too high. "You'll go over the bar!" he'd shouted, as he tramped up the driveway and past her towards the house. As soon as he turned his back, she'd stuck out her tongue. He'd looked back and seen her: he, a black silhouette against the sun, she a blurred bird-like outline, toes still pointing skywards. By the time he'd managed to drag her down for cheeking him, he was ranting in that incoherent state where care and concern turn into rage. "Don't you ever defy me," he shouted and she cried in the gulping, non-comprehending way that she was doing now. "You'll go over the bar," he'd said, but that was what she had wanted to do, because nobody knew what that felt like. Even on the swings in the park, the park ranger shouted the same thing. Sometimes they'd stand on the swing and try to make it go as high as possible, or take a whole line full of them up high on to the big swing boats; flying, flying, always trying to go over the bar.

Kathryn sat in the car back to being a six- or seven-year-old again. She'd taken her father's hand to climb mountains in those days. He and she would take off on Saturdays in a ritual that he supervised from the minute he'd call into her bedroom. "It's a good day for climbing," he'd say and she'd tumble out of bed, feet cold on the bedroom lino, before her toes touched the mat. By the time she got to the kitchen, he would be whistling to himself in the kitchen. It was the only time he ever prepared any food. Clinking eggs would be hard-boiling on the stove, whilst a kettle steamed for a pot of tea. The tea would then be poured into a cream coloured flask with red and green stripes. A small glass bottle of milk stood ready on the kitchen table and daddy would be buttering bread and mashing bananas to spread on the white slices with bright red raspberry jam. The smell of bananas still brought back that steamy kitchen to her. She hopped from foot to foot; "Where are we going today, daddy?"

"Into the far unknown. Troops stand to attention!" She'd stand to attention while everything was packed into his canvas bag, then they'd drive away down the road, just her and him, with mummy standing waving and Kathryn sitting up in the passenger seat. Most times, she didn't even wave back, caught up in their world, heading for the far unknown. In those days, they would drive up into the Mourne Mountains, park the car and climb the nearest peak. One morning, there was still snow lying and they'd seen a fox, russet clear on the white slopes. She'd hardly been able to breathe when it turned its sharp head towards them. They always lifted two stones to put on top of the cairn on the summit. Kathryn liked to choose small white stones that she thought were made of marble, like the beautiful white angels in church. Daddy would put the two stones in the pocket of his prickly tweed jacket and they'd clink together as he and she trudged along, she half-running to keep up with him.

Halfway up, they'd sit down together on a rocky promontory, unpack the sandwiches, bananas now blackened, pour the tea and milk and drink in the clean air. "It's like pure oxygen," he'd always say. She didn't know what that was. Then her daddy would pull two apples out of his pocket, green for him, red for her, polish them on his sleeve and stand up. "Troops stand to attention," he'd say and then they'd go on to the summit. After they put their stones on the cairn, he'd salute. "Ready for the descent, no extra oxygen required on this occasion. Everything shipshape for the return journey?"

"Everything shipshape," she'd say and they'd start their downward climb.

Sometimes, they'd almost break into a trot on the last slope down towards the road. They'd arrive home wind-reddened and starving, happy in their conspiracy of togetherness. Her mother would have shepherd's pie or bacon and tomatoes ready in the oven for them and buttered barmbrack on the table, set out on the white china plate with the gold rim. She knew better then to ask them where they'd been. All she ever said was, "Good day?" Kathryn and her daddy didn't even bother to answer, just nodded and went to the kitchen sink to lather hands and forearms with soap, together, before they sat down at the kitchen table.

She and her father had never gone anywhere together of recent years. Kathryn and her mother would often go shopping on Saturdays, but her father sat in the car, or if he came along he would join the other men loitering outside shops till they emerged. Kathryn couldn't really remember when their days out together had stopped. She'd started to get too busy to go off climbing. Birthday parties had started to take up most Saturdays. Her mother drove her to those and Kathryn hated them. "Postman's Knock" was the favoured game for a while. Some one of the boys would leave the room as the postman. She used to sit in the circle, digging her nails into the palm of her hand, silently praying: "Please God, don't let it be number five. Please God, I promise I will love everybody, even that girl with fat ankles in Primary Seven. Don't let him say number five, God, please."

Kathryn stopped the car outside the wrought iron gates of the Botanic Gardens and went into the Palm House. She buried her head in the white hyacinths until the heady scent seemed like a part of her own being and the hospital smell receded from her nostrils.

That next afternoon, the nurse was beside her father. "Look, here's Kathryn come to see you." She saw an expression of pure joy cross her father's face and then he turned his head round to look at her. His look darkened and he lowered his eyes. "I wasn't the Kathryn you were expecting," she said as she set a pot of white hyacinths on the bedside locker. He didn't look up as she talked of the florist's near her house and the spring flowers that were blossoming everywhere.

When she turned to go, she touched his hand. "I love you daddy." As she walked away, she thought she heard a whisper. "Into the far unknown." When she looked back, he held her gaze for an instant with the most unutterable sadness in his eyes, and the scent of the hyacinths lay heavy in the air.

My Daughter, Oh My Ducats!

by Geraldine Burke

The news spread like wildfire through the village. Almost all the inhabitants experienced the thrill of excitement when they heard that the Master's daughter had run away from home.

It wasn't that they wished any ill to befall Jessica MacArthur; but the village schoolmaster was not a popular man. For one thing, he was excessively vain and made no secret of his disdain for the villagers. When anyone dared to argue with him, he would fly into an uncontrollable rage. Specks of foamy spittle would fly from his mouth and lodge on the spiky ends of his grey moustache. He was on the short side for a man, being about five and half feet tall and rather stringy with it. The butcher remarked that he wouldn't make a decent pot of soup.

My mother heartily detested him. I suspect that they must have crossed swords at some function or other at the Village Hall where each had tried to gain the upper hand. I overheard her telling Miss McClusky, the dressmaker, that the Master was a victim of self-delusion. Miss McClusky eagerly agreed… she agreed with most of my mother's opinions, perhaps because she was the Station Sergeant's wife and as such wielded not a little influence in the village of Ballygudden.

Since we lived in the Police Barracks, we were the first to learn about Jessica's disappearance. My younger sister, Alice, and I shared the bedroom that overlooked the porch. When we heard the iron knocker banging that fateful night, we leaned out dangerously to see who was making such a din. We drew back hastily when we glimpsed the unmistakeable, stringy figure of the Master, illuminated in his night attire by the porch lantern.

Alice giggled, "He looks like a runaway convict…all those stripes!"

I suggested we creep downstairs to hear what was going on

but Mammy forestalled us and sent us scurrying back to bed. In the event, we heard the Master's opening screech, "My darling! My Jessica! You must find her! She's gone…" And then the door shut discreetly and we knew he was being interviewed by my father. Neither of us could sleep from excitement. "Do you suppose Jessica has eloped?" Alice enquired in hopeful tones.

"Of course, you mutt!" I returned obligingly.

Both of us were thinking along the same lines. Master MacArthur's favourite dramatic episode from Shakespeare was JESSICA'S ELOPEMENT. It was also our favourite because it had everything! A runaway romance, a handsome young husband and a lavish spending spree! What girl could ask for more?

And on top of all that, the cruel, mean, old father, Shylock, got his just desserts. I've often thought that the Master must have overlooked the ending!

His younger daughter Daphne was twelve like me. We liked her because she would meet us secretly in the gravedigger's hut for an exchange of information when something exciting happened.

On that momentous day she had plenty to disclose. "Just wait 'til you hear this…" she teased us. "What?" we chorused. "Father's valuable stamp collection is missing from his desk!"

We gasped, thrilled to the marrow. The Master's famous stamps! He was always boasting about their value and relating how his father before him had started the priceless collection. Our local Jessica might not fling ducats from a gondola on a canal in Venice but she could create a few tidal waves with the celebrated stamps.

"Father's convinced that she's gone off with the Squire's son Phillip," Daphne's voice broke in our delighted speculations, "You know that crazy fellow who's always hanging about, making sheep's eyes…"

"No, we noticed nothing…"

"Father found sick-making letters from him in her desk and he's hopping mad. I think he will probably shoot him," announced Daphne happily.

When we finally returned home, it was plain to see that Father was not in a good mood. It seems that the Master had been pestering him practically all day with demands that all vehicles and boats leaving the North of Ireland should be stopped and searched for runaways. Furthermore he insisted that the Squire should be interrogated regarding the movements of his son, Phillip, and that a detailed description of the young man be read out on the wireless. Hadn't he been guilty of abducting his beautiful daughter and purloining a priceless collection of stamps?

The stamps could not be traced once the collection was broken up to be sold off to the highest bidders.

As he left to return to duty, Father said crossly, "I'm beginning to wonder which is more important to him... his daughter or his stamps!"

Later as we ate supper in our kitchen, the Master's wife knocked timidly at the back door. Her face looked very red and she apologized to Mammy for disturbing her so late. "We've found Jessica," she murmured, "She was hiding in the garden-shed all the time. Please tell the Sergeant and thank him for all his patience."

The poor lady sounded really ashamed. Mother told us to finish our biscuits outside.

I was pleased to see Daphne picking blackberries in the churchyard. She was glad to tell us how Jessica had "planted" clues to give the impression that she had eloped with Phillip. She wanted to punish her father for refusing her permission to attend the end-of-term dance without him as chaperone. The masterstroke was to break open the Master's desk to remove the precious stamp collection. For almost twenty-four hours he was left moaning alternately about his missing daughter (defiled?)

and his priceless stamps, doubtless being sold piecemeal by a careless hand to finance the runaways.

I was bitterly disappointed that there had not been an elopement. Since I had never met anyone who had run off to Gretna Green, I'd been looking forward to hearing all the thrilling details, even at second-hand. It was a real letdown to discover that Jessica had travelled no further than the bottom of her father's overgrown garden. But the villagers thought it was the joke of the century and all at the Master's expense!

And, yes, Jessica was given permission to attend the dance without her father. Oddly enough, after that episode, he no longer had the same enthusiasm for Shakespeare.

The Aul Wan

by Lily McWilliams

The aul wan was next door crying her lamps out again on Friday night. She wailed like a banshee rapper. My ma was all annoyed. It stopped her and my Da having their usual Friday night melee.

Last week he hit her. She accused him of looking at somebody else in the club. He went mad running about the house in his boxer shorts banging his fists off the walls. The aul wan must have heard it for her bedroom is connected to my Ma's.

She never lets on the next day and neither do we.

It's all polite stuff about the Grandchildren and who's expecting again. We saw her at the one o'clock mass yesterday. She looked desperate. Her eyes were all red. During the mass she kept her head down. My Ma says it's terrible the way he died so suddenly. Dropping dead in the aul wan's arms. She ran out calling for help. Of all the days my Ma was out. Two men up our road ran in. They locked the aul wan in the parlour. Apparently her Husband was lying haemorrhaging to death on the floor. When I came home from school for my lunch the Police and the Ambulancemen were there.

Then crowds of her ones began to arrive.

When my Ma came home she sat and cried and said he had been a harmless sort of cratur.

They took his body away in the morgue van.

I was watching from our front room window. I felt sick. I told my Ma. She said to stop nosying and keep away from the window. I couldn't though. I was a wee bit traumatised cause the day before the aul wan's Husband had slipped me fifty pence. I begged my Ma to let me stay off school.

She agreed so long as I walked the dog.

The next day a big shiny hearse brought the coffin home. You could hear them all crying next door. It went on for ages. I don't like people crying so me and our dog went up the Cave Hill. I sat there all day looking down all over Belfast. Me and the dog rolled up and down the hills. We were filthy. I wondered about dead people. Their white faces and waxy fingers. I liked the aul wan's youngest son who was away at university in England. My Ma told my Da they were waiting for him to fly home that night.

Everyone had their blinds pulled down. Even Deko's Ma who hated the aul wan. Me and him were both to blame. Last summer we climbed through the aul wan's hedge and Deko got carried away. He set fire to her wheelie bin. She ran out and burned her hands trying to put the fire out. My Da nearly killed me. I was grounded for weeks. The aul wan was connected it seemed for two men from The Ra came to our house and Deko's. They warned us if anything else happened next door that we would be in serious trouble.

Deko's Ma never touched him. I was not allowed near him. He hated that. In school and on the road he started bullying me. I told my Ma. Her and Deko's Ma got stuck into it over our hedge. Nothing stopped him though. When I was out back he would open the attic window and call me all sorts of pervert wankers.

Give him a good dig said my Da and he will soon leave you alone.

Hundreds of mourners came to the aul wan's house for the wake. The road was choc-a-bloc with cars. Deko's Ma was out cursing, demanding to know what effer had blocked her driveway. My Da said some people had no respect.

I saw the youngest Son arriving home. I could not believe that a big fellow like that could cry so much. I hoped my Da would never die and leave us.

I used to watch the aul wan's Husband out in their garden after he got his cancer treatment. He had no hair left. He shuffled about gasping for breath. The weight had fallen off him and he looked like a rake. He was not supposed to smoke any more or so the aul wan told my Ma. But I watched him having a puff behind their garage when she was not around. He caught me on several times and gave me a smile and the thumbs up.

My Ma made a big pot of soup for the wake. To calm her nerves she drank two vodkas. The soup got burnt. I tried to tell her. She shoved me out of the way and said I was worse than a wee girl at times. I asked her could I go to the wake. No way she said. Not after shaming your Da and me. I still felt bad. I wanted to make it up to the aul wan for when she used to go away on her holidays she always brought us rocks and sweets. Our dog was expecting. Maybe I could give her a pup.

You could hear the buzz all night through their walls.

All the tension seemed to drift into our house. I could not sleep. So I got up and went to look out at the back garden. The aul wan was sitting by herself on a bench. She looked lost and lonely. My Ma came in from the wake dead drunk. She grabbed my Da and told him she would love him forever. That if he ever died she could never live without him. He told her to go on up to bed. But secretly he looked dead pleased.

The funeral mass began at nine o'clock. The aul wan and her six children all sat in the front row. Two fellows played a guitar and a flute. The youngest son bowed his head and wept so loud all over the chapel that everyone else was crying as well. The four sons carried him out. They walked down the road again and stopped outside their house for a few minutes.

All the while our dog barked at our front gate. My Ma walloped me across the head and said I should have tied her up.

Then the funeral moved on and they were away for the rest of the day.

My Da said they were a great family with brains to burn. Sure just look at them. All DOCTORS and TEACHERS and SOLICITORS.

Some of them stayed with the aul wan for a month. Then she

was on her own. She had such a forlorn expression though her eyes held a lifetime of memories.

Her garage was broken into. They stole her gardening stuff. My Da said if he caught anyone near her place he would put his boot right up their arses. Then her cats were poisoned.

Someone put a dog's turd through her letterbox. At Hallowe'en fireworks were lit and thrown up her hall. She was like a skeleton with worry. My Ma said this was supposed to be a posh area. God help us if this was what we were living beside.

My Da said did we realise the good neighbour the aul wan was. What if she decided to move and we got a load of riff raff in. The aul wan's sons came and stayed. They caught Deko with a can of petrol on her patio.

There were ructions as the Police took him away. His Ma screamed and said the aul wan had better look out.

What is this road coming to said my Da. I brought youse out of the ghetto to give youse all a chance.

Our houses were big pre-war semi detached with garages and gardens that stretched all the way down seventy foot long gardens at the back onto a river.

I mind the time said my Da when only the really rich could afford to live up here. When I was a wee boy I used to do their paper round. But they were a real stingy crowd. Wouldn't have given you a sixpence. Not even at Christmas. The most I ever got off them was a wee hard bun. I never even ate it. I give it to my dog. They were never known to ate much you know. That's why they had their big fancy houses. Could show all of us how to live.

Nobody's going to buy these big houses said my Ma only big families. Youse are all near reared now and all me and your Da wants is a bit of peace. I shrugged. It was getting very bad what with that crowd selling dope at the corner and them messers up at the disco picking fights for nothing.

As me and my Da cut our hedges he said education is what

will get youse out of here into a better life. Take a leaf out of the aul wan's sons.

Deko was put away indefinitely. Out in the back garden his Ma threw insults over the hedge when she knew the aul wan was there.

I began to make up for the years when I had neglected my education. To my Ma and Da's delight I was third in my exams. The aul wan called me in one day and gave me a box of books. I lost myself in them for hours.

Although she was still living beside us you sensed that change was coming. My Ma started a novena to Saint Jude the Saint of Hopeless People for the aul wan to stay.

In the middle of the night the aul wan was attacked in her home. Deko had escaped and come looking for revenge.

I'm looking at a horde of mad kids rampaging round the aul wan's garden while six adults sit drinking vodka. Three dogs are barking. The place is a kip already with six cars, two caravans and a lorry out at the front and up the driveway.

Our house is all fenced in as well as Deko's Ma's hedge. She is never around. Not since Deko was put in a closed unit. She spends all her days travelling to visit him.

There's no chance these ones will ever move out now says my Da. They have dug themselves too well in. My Ma disagrees saying it is unusual for the travelling people to put down roots like this. The aul wan's children got their own revenge when the house was sold privately. The travellers paid cash up front and got a bargain.

I'm sweating again for my exams just like the aul wan's children used to do.

It doesn't matter who lives next door now.

As far as I'm concerned it will always be the aul wan's house and nobody else's.

The Comedown Queen

by Mary Fitzgerald

It was the sound of track four skipping on the stereo that woke her up.

She didn't know how long the CD had been stuck. Maybe it had been hours. The dull drone of techno strangled mid-track and the same snatch of distorted vocals that escaped from the speakers, only to skip back again, irritated her and made her head pound.

Her body felt hot and tingly. The sticky, sweaty dampness of her skin felt clammy against his. Beads of sweat had collected above her collarbone, under her arms and between her breasts and legs. Wherever her body touched his. Sweat that smelt stale and curiously metallic. A mix of perfume, cigarettes, alcohol, spices from the Indian she had for dinner last night and god knows what else. Chemical sweat.

Her jaws were still chewing the same piece of gum from last night. Her mouth was dry and the tasteless wad of chewing gum was like a ball of rubber bands that her teeth rose and fell on again and again. She turned over and lay on her back. A dull ache crept along her spine from the small of her back up to her neck. It was always like this on Sunday morning.

She always hated the long, slow comedown.

Reaching her arm out from under the blanket, she grappled with the remote control and turned the stereo off. The sudden silence that invaded the small room made the ringing in her ears even louder. She had been dancing next to the club's huge speakers all night. The pounding of the bass deep inside her chest left her breathless and elated. She had felt on top of the world. She had felt like she could do anything.

Running her hands over the bedside table and under the bed, she tried to locate the packet of cigarettes she remembered buying at the 24-hour garage on her way home last night. She found the packet crushed and torn with only one cigarette inside. That meant she would have to go to the shop. Shit. But she knew she couldn't get through the next few hours without them.

She lit her cigarette, took a long drag and inhaled deeply. The blue smoke twisted and swirled, caught in a shaft of morning light that came from the part of the window where the curtains didn't quite meet. The body next to her shifted and still asleep, turned over. She could see his face. He looked different now; almost childlike with the hard lines of his face relaxed. He moved again, the side of his face nestling into the pillow. "Lola", he murmured, his lips forming a half-smile.

Lola liked her name. She remembered some Spanish guy she had met in a bar in town one summer who laughed when she told him her name and told her that all the prostitutes in Spain were called Lola. His name was Pepe and she told him that was a brand of jeans here in Belfast. He didn't laugh.

Lola. Lo. La. Lola. She said her name out loud over and over, rolling her tongue over the round, fleshy vowels. It sounded playful, the two syllables moving together like a seesaw, back and forth. Lo. La.

Of course Lola wasn't her real name. She had changed it when she moved out of home at sixteen. A new name for a new life. She used to sing along to the Kinks song when she was a kid and always thought someone with a name like Lola could never have a humdrum, ordinary life.

Not like the name her parents gave her. Lily. She remembered the moment when she had started to hate her name. Two mothers standing at the school gate with their daughters, her new school friends. "Lily, is it?" they said, smiling down at her. "What a funny old-fashioned name to give a child," she heard them say to each other.

Lily was the name of some of the old ladies with crepe-like

necks and liver-spotted hands who always ordered soft boiled eggs and pots of tea at the café where she worked in the city centre.

Lily was the cloying, sickly-sweet smell of her grandmother's neck when she stood on tiptoes to kiss the mottled and powdered eighty-year-old skin.

Lily reminded her of the white bar of Lily of the Valley soap that always sat on the porcelain soap dish in her grandmother's bathroom. Easter lilies - white and pure. Lily-livered. Lily - old-fashioned, white, pure, virginal, weak. Not like Lola. Lily and Lola. Madonna and Whore.

The cigarette had burned right down to the filter and ash lay scattered and smeared on the blanket. On mornings like this Lola's mind always drifted off. One morning she forgot she was holding a cigarette and burned a hole in the sheet. Another time she accidentally swallowed her last piece of gum and before she knew it, had chewed the inside of her mouth until the skin was broken and bleeding.

Lola looked at the alarm clock. 12.30. It was later than she had thought. She would walk to the shop, buy cigarettes, orange juice and rolling papers and spend the rest of the day in bed.

Swinging her legs slowly out from under the blankets, Lola sat on the bed. The dress and jacket she had worn last night were in a heap on the floor. She picked them up and began to dress herself. The scratchy nylon of the dress felt uncomfortable against her damp skin and the smell of stale cigarette smoke and spilt beer made her feel sick.

She was putting on her jacket when she caught sight of herself in the mirror above the sink. She stepped closer to the surface of the small, stained mirror, a cheap buy from a discount shop in town, and looked closely at her reflection. Her face looked unfamiliar. The skin was grey and seemed to be stretched tightly over her face. In contrast, the skin around her eyes, with their still-dilated pupils, was puffy. The glitter she had painstakingly applied last night had gathered in the wrinkles that ran like rivulets from the corner of her eyes and her tan make-up had slid into the creases around her mouth. She had given up counting wrinkles a long time ago. Three years ago. When she had turned thirty.

Her reflection shocked her. She looked at the woman in the mirror staring back at her. A woman who had spent seventeen years looking for the life she had always dreamed of. A life to fit the name she had chosen for herself. A life that had never happened.

A woman who would work long days at the café and come home, smelling of chip fat and Ulster Fries, to the cramped bed-sit she hated. A woman who pretended to be someone else when an old friend from school recognised her on the street. A woman who went out on a Saturday night to forget what her life had become.

Lola looked over her shoulder at the sleeping figure on her bed, the shape of his body visible through the blankets. She tried to remember his name. Something beginning with C. Chris, Colm, Ciaran...she couldn't remember. She didn't even know his name. It would be the same old story again. The awkwardness, the few stilted attempts at conversation, the coldness of strangers replacing the closeness of the night before. The closeness that feels real but along with everything else always wears off by morning.

He turned in his sleep again. Lola stared at him, at his unfamiliar face buried in the pillow and his arms that clutched the blanket around him.

She had to leave.

Pulling on her boots that reached up to her knees, Lola took one last look around her little flat. She looked at the dirty dishes piled high in the sink. She looked at the photographs in their silver frames on the mantelpiece. Pictures of happier times. Lily with her parents, Lola with some famous DJ at a club in town.

She looked at the overflowing ashtray and the empty bottle of vodka. She stared again at the stranger in her bed before she walked out the door. Lola was leaving and this time she wasn't coming back.

The Saddest Woman I Have Ever Known

by Shannon McLaughlin

Albert's death made no more stir than the fall of a sparrow. After the funeral Peggy sold up and moved to Egypt. People barely raised an eyebrow in surprise. Peggy was always capable of theatrical gestures. She lived on the fringes of lunacy.

"She's a silly old tart," the stalwart matrons of society would chorus and simmer with disapproval. Peggy could never fit into their clean and aggressive respectability. She was a drunk, a debauched and degenerate old broad. She was also the kindest and perhaps the saddest woman I have ever known. Fallen women are the only ones that have good shiny souls.

Peggy had an almost palpable sadness like a miasma surrounding her, a melancholy that smouldered in her small dark eyes. She was always wonderfully garbed with a perpetual hunger to be beautiful and a desperate thirst to be loved. When she put on her make up she felt that she put on her life. She was defining herself with every deft stroke of her eyeliner. Rolling on the crimson red lipstick she gave definition and breathed life into an amorphous face. She would then pout and smile at the mirror. Peggy was conspicuously light hearted. She said that when she was really sad that was when she laughed loudest.

Peggy had a sad, sad life. She had been abandoned by her mother. She was then raised by a series of dutiful yet reluctant aunts.

There was a great void in Peggy's life that her well-meaning relations could not fill. She had a favourite daydream; it was that her mother would come and take her away to her new home in America. Her mother would be dressed in a diaphanous, glamorous gown and be drenched in French perfume. Sometimes she would look like Lana Turner, or whomever Peggy had recently seen in the movies. Peggy would fly away with her mother and sit in a grand restaurant eating Knickerbocker Glories. Sadly, this dream never came true. The reality was that Peggy's mother never came home. She lived in New Jersey with a nasty little Jewish man called Sydney. She had no more children.

When Peggy was seventeen she met Albert. Life was wonderful. She fell in love and, like all women, she surrendered to the very God of Love himself. Whereas Albert, like all men, was only temporarily in love.

Peggy got pregnant. Peggy's aunts, from their vantage point of privileged goodness, nodded their heads and rolled their eyes heavenward and muttered about a bad seed and bad blood. They distanced themselves completely from the scandal and the social disgrace. Albert's family were worse. Albert was part of a large Italian, Catholic family and he was the eldest boy and the dreams and aspirations of the father sat heavily on his shoulders. Albert's mother was inconsolable, almost catatonic.

She was a spiteful old hag and not without subtlety and inventive powers. She called Peggy a schemer and a mongrel that did not even know her own lineage. Peggy did not react to these barbs; besides, the old lady's talons were sharp and glistening with the blood of recent victims. Peggy was terrified by the pregnancy and she assumed all the guilt and she felt sure her mother-in-law was right. Somehow it was all her fault. There are no photographs of the wedding. The young couple emigrated to Canada and sailed away from scandal and controversy.

After six weeks on a ship Peggy wondered what the hell she was doing with this ignorant young boy. A boy who touched her flesh at will, who was rough and coarse and who hurt her and left her feeling sore and discarded. Albert made it clear from the beginning that he felt she had entrapped him; he was unfulfilled and torn away from his ambitions. He was full of anger, jealousy and bitterness and these feelings curdled into a poison. He directed this venom at his young wife. He was needlessly and deliberately cruel.

He called her a little half-breed and a mongrel. He controlled the finances and he controlled the relationship. He was like a little boy who has captured an exotic butterfly and is toying with the idea of ripping off its pretty wings or squashing the fluttering beauty with the flat of his hand.

Life was tough in Canada.

A baby boy was duly born, followed two years later by a baby girl. Their apartment was infested with roaches. Albert could not speak French and could only get a menial job on the railways. The work was hard and thankless and poorly paid. Peggy became pregnant again and Albert seethed with anger.

This time Albert paid for an abortion. Peggy had no remorse: she already had two babies and a life of unrelieved gloom. The abortion was crude and illegal and Peggy haemorrhaged. A hard faced woman named Mrs Foster came to take care of her. Mrs Foster was all stone and iron and no humanity. She drank and she introduced Peggy to the medicinal powers of whiskey.

Whiskey could soothe her. Most of the time, it was her only companion.

Ten years later the couple came home and bought a splendid house in suburbia. They lived unhappily ever after. The children grew up and moved away as soon as possible. Albert and Peggy stayed together. They skirted around each other awkwardly like two lodgers in a guesthouse.

Peggy made three suicide attempts. The first and most serious happened 25 years ago. She cut her wrists. It was the first time she had seen Albert and his lover together. She had been abandoned once again. She had sudden moments of panic when the reality of her life was treacherously revealed to her and she was stunned by sorrow. The thought of death came and stayed with Peggy and lent her vague feelings of happiness and peace. Suicide was an alternative she kept close by to comfort her. If her life became too dreadful she had an alternative.

They stayed together, possibly because they did not know what

else to do and also because Albert did not believe in divorce
- he did not want the social stigma. They both found solace in
different ways. Peggy in drink and Albert with his lover in their
bed of secret joy.

All passion spent they disliked but understood each other
completely.

Peggy had lots of liaisons, usually with burnt out Lotharios
that no other woman would tolerate. Peggy was patient with
men; her patience came from fundamental humility. She petted
men and nurtured their egos. She thirsted after their approval
and attention.

In her haze she never recalled just how many men entered her
life and left it. She always attracted men although she never had
any real affection for any one of them.

I have a photograph of Peggy and Joe; he was one of her litany
of admirers. She was most content with Joe. He was a constant
in her life for two years. She always said she didn't have to force
herself to be happy with Joe. She didn't have to laugh. The
photograph is faded but there is frivolity in the background;
perhaps a wedding party, a funeral, a gathering, an occasion to
drink and forget for a while. Peggy has laced her plump little
arm through Joe's burly one. Her hat is large worn with a rakish
slant. She is wearing her blue-black Elizabeth Taylor wig. Her
blouse is transparent; a vivid rose colour trimmed with yellow
lace, the rouge shrieks from her face and her little dark pebble
eyes are lined with baby blue. She is wearing her long silver
lucky dolphin earrings. Her little plump hands are bejewelled
and her fingernails are varnished bright red. Her face is round
and vast and her mouth, like a little gash, is unskilfully painted
red.

Joe is just like any middle-aged drunk you would find in any
city. He is balding, heavy, with big mauve jowls. His face is shiny
and red; he has a bulbous nose and huge round watery jellyfish
eyes. He is smiling, showing his opaque and lustreless teeth. He

is wearing a white shirt open to the neck, no tie, and his sleeves are casually rolled up; he is sitting a little to the left trying to disguise his paunch.

Joe and Peggy are having a great time; they are raising their glasses to life and love and they gush at the photographer. A frozen moment. All that human misery and sadness captured for eternity.

Peggy would often say to me that no one realised what a tight rope she walked or what would happen if she slipped. The abyss. Despair. All these things. Peggy was kind. Even in her helpless state she always showed humanity and understanding to her friends.

I met Albert before he died. He was a small man, frail, a yellow pallor, his big blue-grey orbs surveying everything, disseminating. I asked about Peggy. He drew in his breath and shrugged his shoulders and said: "Oh you know Peggy! Drinking herself into oblivion as we speak."

I would never be complicit in his denunciation. I would not be a sniggering accomplice.

He always invited public criticism of Peggy: he liked to diminish her. I thought he should have had a modicum of loyalty. Peggy joked about Albert and his rituals and his meticulous ways. She loved to talk about his pathological hatred of disorder and dust. Every evening prior to visiting his lover Albert showered and changed. Peggy called this "The Washing of the Balls ceremony". Peggy was a master storyteller and we would howl with laughter and beg her to tell us about the time she did this or that. She delivered these tales like a professional. She had her little repertoire, which she told through various stages of the evening. Peggy knew her audience and could decide which story would be suitable. But as she said, when people laugh loudest that is when they are saddest. She always acknowledged the fact that Albert had another partner, although she never betrayed his secret.

When Albert was dying Peggy was very attentive and conscientious in his care. She stopped drinking and fetched all his needs. She agreed with Albert's lover that visits could be made. Everything was very civilised and modern. Albert was afraid to die. He was tortured by visions of hell and of all the sins he had committed in this world. Peggy was holding his hand when he died.

Peggy now had money for the first time in her life. Albert had kept her in near penury. He had kept her on a leash. His only vestige of control. She had always wanted to travel and she decided to go on a cruise on the Nile.

I received a postcard a few months later of the inscrutable sphinx. She informed me that the money was still lasting and that she had fallen in love. There was a garbled note about a travel guide named Bepo and a great red moon detaching itself from a charcoal sky. I smiled as I thought of Peggy sitting in a little bar in Cairo laughing and enchanting people with her funny tales.

Next thing I heard was that Peggy had sold up and moved to Egypt, to Cairo.

She sent me some photographs.

Peggy and Bepo by the Pyramids, Peggy by the Pyramids, the Sphinx. Peggy's fat little feet sinking into the warm, soft sand and her silver dolphin earring catching the light. She is wearing a blazing orange dress, which is taut across her chubby body; she has topped it all with her jet-black wig.

She looks like a fat bumblebee.

She has a cigarette in one hand and her other hand is across her eyes, shielding herself against the strong sun. She is smiling, fan shaped wrinkles rest under her dark little eyes. There is a cloud of sadness and fatigue engulfing her. The other photo is of Peggy and Bepo, he is a mulatto Adonis smiling knowingly at both Peggy and the photographer.

They are raising a glass at a wedding, at a party, a funeral in a place you can drink and forget a while. They are toasting life, love and hope.

God help them.

A forlorn figure, Albert's lover fastidiously tends his grave.

He is a fine boned pretty little man with prominent eyes. He has dressed with care; a pork pie hat is perched on his head, no doubt to cover a baldpate.

He has lost his lover. He is beyond sadness; he is broken hearted.

Carnival

by Sonia Haddad

We are in Marseilles at a time between sun glare and Mistral wind. Lent is bowing in, but for now, we are in Carnival mood.

A long-haired youth with a cigarette dangling from his lips, hands us flyers promoting a 'Boum Mardi Gras'. As we move along the Rue de Rome, someone else hands us another 'Super Party'.

He wraps his arms around me, making it difficult to walk until I find his rhythm, and then we swing along down La Canebière. We're going to see a film, *Autour de Minuit*. I've already bought the music in the FNAC. As a souvenir.

I've been following him about for some time now: Paris, Scotland, Marseilles. Marseilles is my favourite place and he may stay here longer because of the work.

I might lose my own job.

Maggie has been ringing the flat in Lexham, wanting to know if I feel better, if I can come to the phone. But I'm miles away in the Hotel Saint Anne, Rue de Coteau. With him.

I tell him I might lose my job but he takes me to Dessanges after the film and I come out with a French hair cut, short and chic the way he likes it, like red nails and Ebène de Balmain.

We buy two large Pan Bagnats on the street. "We're so lucky," he tells me and I believe him because he is the man of my dreams and I am with him.

I feel hungry and look forward to eating the Pan Bagnat but he takes it out of my hand before I even get to bite and hands it over to a begging tramp. He is so smug with his saintly act, not even bothering to turn around; but I do. I see our favoured tramp spit on the ground in disgust and throw the sandwich away.

He's going through a benevolent phase and I follow because

I know he is a man of many phases like the moon, sometimes lunatic and open to prediction, but there is always the inevitability that a phase will pass and a new mania grip him.

I'm still lucky.

We stroll around the Parc Borely in spite of the biting wind and one of the gardeners offers me a beautiful yellow rose that I will keep and press and treasure because he was with me. As the weak sun sinks over rust coloured rooftops we catch a bus, singing *La Vie En Rose,* while we get on. An old lady in black smiles and sighs "Ah, les jeunes amoureux!" We get off at Le Vieux Port, which still smells of fish and sea urchins but the fish vendors, women with red faces and muscular voices have gone by now. We are wrapped together and head across to the Entrecôte restaurant.

I like to look at him across a table with a glass of rosé wine in my hand. I like the way he looks at me and I feel glamorous and romantic. I run my fingers through my new hair that I still haven't properly looked at yet. I want to go and look but I can't leave him. Slowly he's absorbing more and more of me. I am diluting myself into him, allowing him to conquer and rule me.

Am I lucky?

The waitress is very pretty and he makes eyes at her, flirts with her, and asks her about getting to the Carnival.

"I was only finding out where to go," he says but has that smug look again. Everybody loves him. It makes me nervous.

We walk back to the Hotel Sainte Anne and I want to stay in. It's our last night for a few weeks until I get back but he wants to go out. "It's Carnival. We can't stay in."

He wants to enter into the spirit by getting dressed up in silly clothes, putting on garish make-up. I argue against it but he insists and he wears me down until I am helping him get dressed and putting stuff on his face and taking photos and laughing and drinking cheap rosé because we are together and I snap with my camera trying to capture him.

The way he has captured me.

We head out into the night. The Mistral has gone and the air is softer and calm. We head down past Le Vieux Port and he looks in at Entrecôte where we both see the waitress taking someone's order with her notepad and I'm glad she can't go to any carnival.

I might lose my job.

"Get one here and stay with me," he says while my heart pounds and races and soars beyond the Chateau D'If in a trance of joy. I'm already living out Maggie's face when I hand in my notice. Already glimpsing our future.

On we walk, wrapped together looking for the Carnival. Most people are going up La Canebière, so we follow. The crowds are laughing and happy; they wave at us and smile, wishing us a joyous Mardi Gras.

We cross another street and find Le Guepard. Loud jazz is playing, drawing us, enchanting us to go in for another round of rosé, then another, which makes me want to declare love and joy but I hold back, afraid it might all disappear if I break the spell.

He holds my hand and kisses me and tells me I am beautiful. "Let's find the Carnival, shall we?"

I don't want to leave the comfort of Le Guepard and its music, others are dressed up too and the atmosphere is warm and friendly but we head out again and the air feels cooler.

We did not expect to encounter a group of Marseillais youth, escaping their tower blocks out by La Rose, where the police don't like to go. They surround us, boiling with boredom, mocking and jeering and calling him names.

I'd warned him.

I'd said, "This is Marseilles," back within the faded walls of Sainte Anne. But he wouldn't listen. Everyone loves him no matter what. Wasn't that it?

The air, the wine, the faraway noise of people having fun, it is spinning in my head when they start to fight.

Fisticuffs is an old-fashioned word but the only one to describe the ensuing scuffle that takes place in front of me. His ludicrous appearance and, I now see it as ludicrous, is offending their narrow maleness. They cannot understand it so they want to destroy it. They call him more names and spit viciously, which reminds me of the ungrateful tramp, the wasted sandwich.

Someone throws a hard punch to his nose, which bleeds a bit. Some girls run up shouting at the youths, perhaps their girlfriends? I recognise the waitress, now changed in mini skirt and high heels. She didn't have to work after all. The girls pull the boys away and I wipe his nose because it is the right thing to do. "Let's go back to the hotel," I say.

For once, he agrees but it is too late. Too late to listen to me. The glamour has been punched out in a single blow.

I want to be me again. I like me.

Maybe he is so handsome, so tempting and lovely like a box of soft caramels. Maybe it would be easier to carry on.

We've missed the Carnival this year.

I look out from the Hotel Sainte Anne, down past Le Vieux Port where the Mistral starts to pick up again, blowing in the chill of Lent.

And I give him up.

For good.

Proper People

by Lily McWilliams

That summer as the school holidays arrived, my father announced that I was going to work for Mrs D, the publican's wife. They owned extensive premises at the bottom of our street.

I listened with dread as my mother said that Mrs D has a baby every year. That she had already had three miscarriages, and God help her, she had her hands full. I was a wee slip of a thing, nervous and quite shy by nature. The thought of what her house would entail filled me with complete terror.

Their living quarters consisted of huge rooms filled with antique furniture. Compared to our small parlour house it was like a palace. On my first morning Mrs D greeted me and brought me in. Her stomach was huge, so another baby was obviously on the way. It was a madhouse full of toddlers and older children, as well as the eldest daughter, the dreaded Olivia, who swept past everyone in the street as though we were a piece of dog's dirt. She ignored me completely as my daily routine fell into the hours of long hard work. Mr D was a pink-skinned portly man whose motto in life, as he constantly reminded everyone, was to "eat well, sleep well, and to * * * * well." I knew this was a coarse expression for he always guldered with laughter at the last reference.

All their relatives and friends were well to do, owning pubs and bars in the centre of Belfast. They lived on the Malone Road and talked all posh, and arrived in fancy cars and talked about their money, their maids and their lifestyles which seemed far above Mrs D's.

Mr D had a spinster sister who helped in the pub. She was a tiny sour-faced woman who peered out at the world from behind silver-rimmed glasses. Olivia was always ignorant with her when the pair of them were behind the counter pulling pints and half un's. On a Saturday night Mrs D entertained. Father Rogan, the parish priest, always came, along with Aunt May from the Malone Road and her bachelor son Gerard. He was a tall, handsome fellow and many a time when I was up the stairs in the washroom he would slip in, give me half a crown and hold me close, nearly squeezing the life out of me. Sometimes he might kiss me, his face flushed and his eyes a bit wild looking. I was so terrified that I just stood there until he left. The half crowns mounted up with the measly wages Mrs D was paying me. Up in our house I hid the money and dreamed about all the things I was going to buy for Christmas.

In their drawing room on the first landing there was a piano with a photo of Mrs D when she was young. After a music lesson Olivia practised and sounded like a banshee on the back wall. Even her father tut-tutted and said he was wasting good money. Another older sister called Theresa was being paid for at a local Catholic college. Once her father asked me some questions from her homework. When I answered them correctly he threw the book at her and called her a stupid dunce. As well as her music lessons, Olivia was taking ballroom lessons in the big bedroom where her parents slept. Her partner was her cousin Gerard. Once I looked in and he was giving her a kiss. When she caught me on she screamed and said I was a nosey wee bitch. After that I always avoided going upstairs whenever she was there.

One morning I arrived to find the house in real pandemonium. Mrs D was in the hospital. Mr D was going ballistic with having the pub to run and all the children to care for. As I fed and washed the wee ones, Olivia and him wrote out the weekly shopping, then she agreed to go with me to the main shop in York Street.

I reached the list to Mr Topping the grocer. Mrs D was his best customer so he gave Olivia and me an apple. He filled box after box with messages and said they would be delivered the same day, and then he asked us for the money.

"Give it to him," ordered Olivia. I stood there shaking. "I haven't got it," I told her. "Liar, liar!" she shouted, "you're a thief, you've stole our money." I began to cry as Mr Topping looked down on me. I kept shaking my head, saying, "I don't have it, I don't." Olivia nipped my arm viciously and shook me like a rag doll. "Youse've never had money, so you stole ours." I was now wailing in real fear, knowing that if such a terrible thing ever got out about me I would be so ashamed. The more I cried, the more fiercely she harassed me, with Mr Topping saying, "Leave her alone, Olivia, the girl says she hasn't got it, so why not go and look for it; maybe you've dropped the purse."

I suddenly remembered the old fashioned things my father had taught us. All his life he said: "Remember, your good name is the only thing you ever really own. Never let anyone take it away."

In that moment I realised what his words meant. In an instant I grabbed Olivia. I swung her round by her long red hair and slapped her till she begged for mercy. Mr Topping came out from behind the counter to separate us. As he did so, Olivia escaped. I ran after her like a mad bull and caught her at the top of our street where I pushed her all the way down to her house; all the while I kept hitting her. The minute we reached her house she rushed inside, yelling for her Da.

He appeared from inside the house and angrily grabbed me and proceeded to search me from head to toe. He believed that I had stolen their money; while I stood there trembling and intensely embarrassed, telling him I never touched the purse. At that, I broke free from his grip and I ran back up to our house.

I almost fell through the door, spluttering and trying to tell someone what had happened. My mother looked so hurt, for she had reared us so well and this accusation was a blemish on her character, and my father's also. She gave me a cup of milk and a biscuit. Some of my relatives who lived in our street came in. One of them was big Eileen who feared no one. "I'll go down and wipe the street with him," she said, but my mother, who was quiet and refined, shook her head and said, "Leave it for now. Her father will sort it out when he comes home." All our ones spoiled me all that afternoon. But deep down, I was wounded.

At teatime, having his supper, my father listened and said little. Afterwards he smoked his pipe and listened to the news on the radio. To cheer me up, our Mona said she would put my hair in pipe cleaners and that I'd have lovely curls the next day. Our Marie lent me a handbag and said I could borrow it anytime. Then, to our horror, big Eileen came in again. She was drunk and raving mad, saying, "We are the most respectable people in the docks. How dare that country bum call me a thief." She smoked ten fags and gulped from a wee half un of whiskey. My mother looked distracted in case the 'big lady', as we called her, lost her head and wanted a fight with Mr D.

"Them people are dirt," shouted Big Eileen. "Sure, they wouldn't pay their maker unless they had to. I know their form. I worked down there cleaning for her as well. They think we are dirt because we're poor." My father smoked his pipe and nodded in agreement.

Big Eileen left and said she would come back later on.

A rap came to our door. Mr D was standing there with a box of buns. "I've come to apologise to the girl," he said. "You see, with all the fuss this morning, with my wife taking sick and all, I forgot to put the purse in along with the shopping list. I brought youse a box of buns."

My father stood back and said quietly: "Get away from my door and take your buns with you." Mr D slunk away and we went inside and shut the door.

In time, our street was demolished to make way for the inner city ring road. Times changed and we all grew up. Yet, to this day, the accusation still stings as I find I still compare their way of life and ours, and I think that we were the better people. We had nothing in those days, and yet it seems now we had everything.

Relief

by Jennifer Hampton

Jacqueleen ran her thumb around her waistline, placing it between her skin and the rim of her maroon school skirt as a measure of detecting any weight gain or loss.

She had accidentally fastened her stripy maroon and grey tie into a tight knot having been preoccupied with the issue of whether or not to have breakfast; she didn't feel hungry, so she decided to skip it yet another morning. As a consequence of this internal monologue her tie now appeared as a demented little knot the size of a walnut. No one else was up in the house; Jacqueleen was the first to leave in the mornings, having passed her 11+ and, to the immense pride of her family, went to a grammar school an hour's journey from the village. When the noisy Ulster Bus finally pulled in beside her house - there was no bus stop in this scattered County Fermanagh, ever-increasing hamlet where the O'Higgins family lived – she fell in beside Bronagh, the driver having kindly jolted the gears or whatever he did to make the bus hiccup like that.

"Are you nervous?" Bronagh enquired of her best friend. "My tummy feels a bit funny, but it could just be my skirt cutting into me; do you ever wish you could cook your own food, Bronagh?"

"No, not really," Bronagh replied, not particularly interested as she was purging her blazer pocket of bus tickets, receipts and Wrigley's wrappers; "Why would you want to cook your own food anyway? Miss McMillan better give me back my mobile today, I can't believe she took it off me."

Jacqueleen had just discovered a small hole in her tights just below her skirt line and was pulling at it so her skirt might cover it, "Just so you could, I don't know, eat what you wanted, follow your own diet, you know what I mean; anyway Bronagh, you were sending a text message in the middle of class."

"Then, Miss Goody Two Shoes, why don't you just make your own food?"

"I can't afford to buy the food I'm talking about; you know, like really healthy stuff." In the course of the conversation, Jacqueleen had managed to substantially increase the circumference of the hole and encourage the growth of an eight-millimetre wide ladder.

"Anyway, what about your speech," Bronagh asked her friend, not wanting to indulge another of these conversations that would inevitably lead to her having to reassure her bus partner that she was not fat and had not put on any weight.

Jacqueleen was to take part in a debate on the Gore / Bush presidential campaign; of course, she was on the Gore side. Most of the girls didn't even know the difference, but she had informed them he was the lesser of two evils. She was undoubtedly the most well informed and intelligent of the four girls she had been friends with since she began her grammar school career. Jacqueleen had a kind of semi-awareness of this, not really believing it all of the time; a C- was enough to convince her otherwise.

Sitting down meant her maroon skirt felt tighter around her waist; this irritated her and she in turn irritated Bronagh as she kept shifting about, attempting to straighten her back and let the skirt slip down slightly, like it would if she lost a few pounds.

The bus driver, seemingly bent on startling the girls, jolted into the bus stop and they entered the gates of St. Cecilia's, the well-thought-of Catholic Grammar where both girls were studying for their A Levels.

Jacqueleen stood up to present her argument, her back again rigid so her nylon skirt fell lower on her hips and hid the flesh uncovered by the hole in her tights. She spoke eloquently and passionately, much to the delight of her Politics teacher. However, in making her way back to her seat, the confident strides she assumed had hitched her skirt up, revealing to the assembly hall, gathered in which were 100 young men from the neighbouring boys' grammar school, the hole and ever-increasing ladder.

She joined the rest of the girls; her team quietly whispered 'well done' as John Paul from St Malachy's extolled the virtues of Bush's tax plans. Jacqueleen, in the relief of finishing, forgot to wish Mary, next to speak, 'good luck'. She squeezed her sweaty hands in disgust at this neglect of manners, her face reddened, her crossed legs exposed the hole even more as her flesh protruded out like a soft button.

So, after eating a canteen-prepared lunch and an array of corn flavoured snacks from St Cecilia's tuck shop, Jacqueleen walked to the science block; these were guaranteed to be empty at lunch time as this area was strictly out of bounds to the lower school, except with supervision.

She lifted the toilet seat, the vigorously washed her hands; she let the cold water run and inserted into the stream her two longest fingers. Not drying them, she walked over to the toilet, still letting the tap run as to avoid any over-zealous science students overhearing any involuntary noises her body might make.

Bending over, she swallowed her fingers and began to feel a little bit better about the hole in her tights.

Revelations

by Rosie Akeroyd

"Karen Robinson, now there's a fine-looking girl, but she's a bit of a quiet type.

"She never comes out except on Sundays, she always has Kevin by her side.

"She's just suffered a miscarriage. Poor woman, of course it must have been terrible, but mind, she won't talk to any of *us*. It must weight heavily on Kevin, just think of the strain, but ach, he's bearing up well.

"Now Kevin, there's a decent man for you. He's so thoughtful and talented, he works very hard to give Karen a nice home, but he always finds time – and money – for the church. I don't mind telling you the leadership has big plans in store for *him*."

Karen Robinson, now there's a fine looking girl, she's a bit of a quiet type. It isn't her choice, it's not like her at all, but it's better that way in the end.

She never comes out, except on Sundays; she always has Kevin by her side. She'd like to join the netball club, and the Bible study group if she could, but she knows that she'll never get the chance.

She's just suffered a miscarriage. Poor woman, of course it must have been terrible, but mind she won't talk of any of *them*. How could she, when all she hears is "it must weigh heavily on Kevin, just think of the strain, but ach, he's bearing up well."

He was clever. The bruises never showed, although more than once she'd had to wear thick tights to be sure. He'd never broken her arm or anything like that and when Sunday came she would always wear make-up to put colour in her cheeks if she needed to.

He'd been excited about the baby, he'd kissed her and hugged her, and just for a while she thought he had learned to keep his temper under control. She'd slowly started to relax again and risk making jokes and comments like she used to. Until the night Tom Redbourne dropped by with a leaflet about the Bible study group. He'd seen Karen reading the poster on the notice board at church but before he could speak to her Kevin had returned from the Gents and she'd turned away.

Tom didn't get to see Karen that night. Kevin always answered the door when he was home. Karen was a bit tired just then; she wouldn't be coming along, but how about a game of squash sometime?

Then the door clicked shut, a car's wheels spun on the gravel and Kevin walked into the kitchen. He laid the folded sheets of A4 paper on the breakfast bar and then calmly climbed the stairs to the bedroom to where Karen was hanging up his work clothes.

He stood still for just a second and watched her. Then he pulled the suit away, swung her round and flung her face down onto the bed. Kneeling over her, he grabbed her hair and pulled it back from her face, hard, until he could see her wincing with pain.

"Did you think I wouldn't find out, eh? Is that what you thought? Wish I'd come home from work a little later tonight, eh?"

Still grabbing her by the hair, he pulled her off the bed and began dragging her across the floor to the landing. Karen, half-crawling, half-lying, tried desperately to haul herself high enough so she could bear the pain in her head but he was dragging her to fast, across the landing now, towards the stairs.

"Please love, I have no idea what you talking about, please believe me, you're hurting me, you're hurting me!" Karen started to scream as she saw the stairs loom large before her.

Now he was dragging her down them... thud... thud... so that her face banged into the banisters. She reached out for his legs just to try and support herself but he stamped on first one hand

and then the other before taking the stairs now two at a time.

Karen crumpled into the foetal position as Kevin let go at the bottom, but only just so that he could yank her arm behind her back and pull her sharply up on to her feet. She screamed out in pain as he shoved her in front of him towards the kitchen, finally slamming her head down on the granite surface of the breakfast bar beside the Bible study leaflet.

"See this can you? See this? Were you gonna tell me about it then, were you? Or were you hoping he'd have come around before I came home from work? You dirty little *slut.*" By now Karen was whimpering in pain and fear, blood running from her nostrils as she tried to focus on the A4 sheets.

"Thought you could get away with it did you? Thought you could get away from *me* and study Revelation with Tom Redbourne, did you, did you?"

He pulled her sharply back from the bar and threw her on the hard, cold tiles. Then he grabbed the leaflet and ripped it into shreds in front of her as she quivered and gasped on the floor.

"Ha! That's the last you'll see of that, you cow," and he started shoving his foot, hard, into her stomach.

"You're a *slut,* everybody knows that, Tom Redbourne knows that, do you hear that? You're nothing but a *slut.*"

He had a rhythm now; the kicks were flying at her abdomen like blows into a boxer's punch-bag. Karen was barely conscious, she could hardly raise her arms as she tried in vain to stave off the wave of attacks on her body, but as she gradually resisted less and less the kicks grew weaker, and slower, until Kevin too was not attacking but kneeling on the floor, weeping.

Now he was running his hands through her hair, again and again, barely able to see through his tears his crumpled, broken mass that was his wife and child.

"Oh Karen, oh Karen," he sobbed uncontrollably as the weight of his hatred and jealousy ebbed from his trembling limbs. "Karen what have I done to you?" Slowly he crawled towards his wife, holding out his hands to caress her face and stroke her hair.

She stiffened, uncertain how to respond. Yet she feared his reaction if she didn't. Watching closely his every move and eye movement, she inched her hand slowly towards his, shakily brushing his hand as it cradled her face, barely able to believe this was happening yet willing it to be OK, God, please let this be OK. And they lay together on the floor and wept.

Karen lost the baby. Kevin wouldn't let her go to the hospital but the GP confirmed what she already knew. She told Kevin the next night after he came in from work. He said nothing; he just picked up his squash gear and grabbed his car keys. He turned to her for a split second, blaming her with his eyes. Then the door slammed shut behind him.

Karen walked back into the kitchen, wrung out her cloth and continued mopping up the blood.

"Karen Robinson, now there's a fine looking girl, but she's a bit of a quiet type.

"She's just suffered a miscarriage, poor woman, of course it must have been terrible, but mind, she won't talk to any of *us*. It must weigh heavily on Kevin; just think of the strain, but ach, he's bearing up well.

"Now there's a decent man for you. He's so thoughtful and talented. I don't mind telling you the leadership has big plans in store for *him*."

Silent Call

by Teresa Davey

The sounds of merriment drifted around her as she lay on the bed. She felt a weight keeping her there, holding her down, even though she was free to go wherever the fancy took her. She just needed to decide where to go.

As the strains of *Auld Lang Syne* echoed around the hostel, seeming to bounce off the walls and ceilings, she reached for her mobile. Just holding it made her feel slightly better. She had to talk to someone but it had to be a person not caught up in the madness that marked this meeting of two years. She punched in a number. She heard it ring once, twice and then halfway through the third ring the phone was lifted. She heard the voice, soft but clear.

"The Samaritans, can I help you?"

She waited, not yet ready to talk but taking in the sound of the voice, attempting to visualise the person who had answered her call. The voice was female, the accent she thought Scottish, reminding her of heather and large areas of hillside overlooking mysterious lochs. Reminding her of the grandparents she had holidayed with when she was a young child and which now seemed a lifetime ago. Reminding her of Calum, a Scottish boy she had once known. She realised now that his wish to remain free was not down to something lacking in her but because his landscape was etched in the blood running through his veins.

"Hello, this is the Samaritans, can I help you?"

The casualness in the tone of voice caught her attention. The person at the other end did not mind if she took her time to reply, was not going to bully her to do or say something she did not wish. Not like Zero, bullying, bullying, always bullying, as though he owned her, which he thought he did.

Zero, whom it has taken all her strength to leave.

"You're through to the Samaritans, just take your time, there's no rush, I'm not going anywhere."

Oh yes. They all say that to begin with, until they have you where they want you. Then it's all action as they get on with what they want. Funny, the only person who was never in a rush to get away was Calum, the boy who needed his freedom, who did not want to make her promise anything.

"My name is Morag, would you like to tell me yours?" asked the voice.

Morag, she thought to herself; now that's what I call a name. A name that sounded as though it belonged somewhere, not like Tracy. Where had Tracy come from, for God's sake? What has caused her mother to give her a name with no sense of family or history about it? When she was gone it would sink without trace. She grimaced and muttered to herself, 'Tracy, you'll sink without trace if you're not careful'.

"Would you like to tell me your name?" Morag's voice enquired once more. "You don't have to, of course, just if you feel like doing so."

Tracy lay there nursing the mobile. No, she didn't feel like telling someone called Morag that her name was Tracy. How she yearned for a strong, no-nonsense name. If she'd had such a name would her life have been the same? If she'd been called Morag, would she have been happy with Calum's love and no promises? If she'd been called Morag would Zero have thought twice about how he treated her? Would he have recognised her inner strength and given her respect? Did something tell him that someone called Tracy was powerless to control her own destiny?

"I know it's difficult to find the right words," Morag continued quietly, "But I'm still here."

It's difficult alright, thought Tracy, sometimes, no matter what you try to say it comes out meaning something else.

I wonder if that ever happens to you, Morag? Perhaps it happens to everyone; perhaps it's the downside of language. She vaguely remembered hearing that there was one language that had many words to describe the one word love. It followed then that some languages must be better than others. She wondered would that make life a whole lot easier, less confusing, or would it only mean more lies? Perhaps if she'd had a better education she could work it out. Yes, she reflected, if she'd been called Morag and had a better education she might have done better.

"Has something in particular upset you that you'd like to talk about?" she heard Morag asking.

You could say that. It could be described as something in particular; in fact it was very particular. He was a real bastard but then perhaps that wasn't totally his fault either. Perhaps he'd never had a mother like Morag. He certainly didn't have a name like Calum that set him at ease with himself. He preferred a nickname that distanced him from reality. No, she didn't want to think of his name, she didn't want to think of his face, she never wanted to see him again.

"I'm still here if you'd like to talk to me," Morag reassured her.

God, it must be a gift to be so patient and not take it personally if someone did not want to respond. She couldn't imagine Morag yelling 'stop wasting my fucking time will you, you fucking waste of space'. If only she had walked away, if only she was Morag with an education, if only his mother had been like Morag. Why hadn't she understood all of this before?

"Are you finding it hard to cope with this being New Year's Eve?" queried Morag.

Hm, Tracy thought, you bet I am. What's so special about a new year if it's not going to be different from the last? It would be madness to celebrate now anyway, it would be too soon.

It might help me to forget for a few hours but I need to forget big time. The truth is I want a fresh start, a new life.

"This is a difficult time for many people," Morag continued.

'A difficult time', what an understatement that was. Yes, this was a difficult time alright. Perhaps many people did have problems as bad as hers but tonight she was on her own, except for you, she added reluctantly as she patted her tummy. Why had she stayed with him so long? He'd left her with no option this time once the kicking started, once he began to kick her baby. How had it come to that stage, though? Why hadn't she realised long ago that he'd never known anyone like Morag?

"I'll listen if you wish to talk," she heard Morag telling her.

As Tracy lay there she felt her unborn daughter moving within her. With her free hand she sought to caress her child through the taut layers of skin that separated them. The movement stopped momentarily as though in response to her touch before continuing again more vigorously. She watched as her growing bump reacted visibly to the force of tiny limbs on the move. It was as though her unborn child was engaged in a battle with the heavy weight that held her in its grip.

"Sometimes it does help to share a problem," Morag gently urged.

As her child rested once more, the first stirrings of hope began to surface within her. There was a decent future waiting for them both. It was there for the taking. A growing confidence began to fill her mind. She would name her daughter Morag to give her a sense of belonging. She would tell her of her grandparents and the land that had been their home. She would get herself an education so that she could help Morag shape her own world. Her child would be brought up well. Something good would come from that poor sod who'd never had a mother called Morag.

Tracy smiled for the first time in many months, if not years.

She patted her baby and hummed a lullaby.

"Are you suicidal?" she heard Morag ask calmly.

Tracy put down the phone. "Thank you for talking to me, Morag," she whispered.

"Morag... Morag... Morag," she continued, her voice growing in strength. Yes, there was something in that name that even now was putting down strong roots.

Swan Lake

by Heather Richardson

Going wrong was easy. Adam was surprised.

He just waited for Mrs Devlin to finish her lecture on all the dangers they would encounter if they strayed from the main shopping street. The other kids had already gathered into groups, in that effortless way they had. He stepped back into a doorway and watched as they drifted away. No one was looking for him. Then he took the street map from his coat pocket and worked out how to get to the railway station.

It had been simple until he stood on the platform looking at the train. The doors were all closed. Inside the dim carriage directly in front of him an elderly woman slowly swept the floor. A few other passengers stood, waiting. They didn't seem patient, more resigned. One of them, a young soldier, looked directly into Adam's eyes for a moment, then turned away. Adam thought that maybe he'd just wait until the train left. Then the great engine coughed into life, and one by one the carriages lit up. The passengers paused for a moment, as if waiting for permission to climb on board. Adam didn't know if some signal had been given, but everyone stepped forward at the same time. He hesitated.

"Better get a move on honey, if you're going."

He stepped onto the train, moving away from the woman's sweet breath, and the pressure of her hand on the small of his back. She followed him. He could hear the rustling of her clothes as he walked along the corridor, looking for an empty carriage. "It's filling up," she said, then, "Hey, we're in luck. Let's go in this one." Adam did as he was told.

He sat down and watched her as she swung a beige leatherette weekend case up onto the luggage rack. Underneath her lightweight raincoat she was wearing a long cream satin dress.

The hem must have been trailing on the station floor. A grey tidemark of damp had wicked upwards through the fabric.

Adam knew about wedding dresses. The bills were paid with the money his mother made from dressmaking. That was how she'd paid for this school trip. She specialised in wedding dresses. Adam hated the way she clamped her lips closed on the glinting rows of pins, holding in the bitter words of discouragement that filled her mouth like bile. Her skill was creating dresses to flatter the shapeless young women who had already spent fruitless hours trying on ready-made gowns in the bridal shops. They liked to go abroad for their weddings these days. Under white pagodas in the Caribbean they stood, those lonely bridges, smoothing silk-satin or sateen skirts over their flaring thighs, pining for mothers and best friends who were too many thousand miles away, wishing someone would tell them they looked lovely, even if it was a lie.

The woman who had forced him onto the train sat now, smiled at him briefly, then rummaged in her shoulder bag. She pulled out a copy of *USA Today,* and began to study it. Adam realised he had been holding his breath. He relaxed a little, and looked out the window at the quiet platform. There were fashions in wedding dresses, Adam knew this. Raw silk was out of favour now. Rich creamy satins were all the rage since Posh and Becks. He wondered if Americans knew about Posh and Becks.

The train gave a soft lurch and began to move out of the station.

"On our way, honey," the woman said, putting her paper down. "Are you English?"

"Irish," Adam said.

"I'm American," she said, unnecessarily. "From a little place called Zennor, Massachusetts. Ever heard of it?" Adam shook his head.

A shadow moved in the corridor outside their carriage. They

both looked up as the soldier Adam had noticed on the platform stepped in. He carried a smell with him, of too many cigarettes and not enough soap and hot water. He sat in the corner, near the door. The train moved off.

No one spoke. Adam took his Walkman from his pocket and slipped in a CD. He was aware of the soldier watching him as he adjusted his earphones. It was easier to close his eyes. The opening bars of *Eugeny Onegin* played clearly in his head. It made him feel dizzy, the way it always did. Adam remembered the first time he'd heard someone play the violin.

He couldn't have been more than three. Not tall enough to look over the fence into next-door's garden. It had been summer, and the grass had brushed high around his bare legs. His father was a reluctant gardener. Little black flies had swooped up from the grass as he toddled along. Then, through the open window of the house next door he heard it. Young as he was, he knew that the simple tune was being played badly. It seemed to stumble forward, note bumping into note, then a clumsy pause before proceeding. But the marvel of it was someone was actually making the sound, creating it the very moment it was heard. Until that day Adam had thought of music as something that happened when his mother turned the radio on. He hadn't realised it could be made.

A hand rested heavily on his shoulder and he jumped. He looked up at a stocky man in uniform who began to talk rapidly in Russian.

"He's checking the tickets," said the American woman. Adam switched his Walkman off and fumbled for his ticket in the back pocket of his jeans. The man studied it, and began shaking his head and talking again.

"I'm sorry, I don't understand, *nyeht. Ahngleeyskee?*" He felt a desperate heat in his face. There was a falling sensation in his stomach.

"I think you're on the wrong train, honey," the woman said,

"this one's going to Archangel, not St Petersburg." She turned to the ticket inspector and talked to him in confident Russian. He seemed to argue with her, then shrugged his shoulders and stepped out of the carriage. The woman leaned over and patted Adam on the knee. "Don't worry, they'll have to do something with you. I mean, they can't throw you off an express train, can they?"

Adam settled back into his seat, his panic subsiding into a kind of tense acceptance. There was nothing he could do to change things. He wondered if Mrs Devlin had realised yet that he was missing. Authorities would be called. He would be found, somehow. Still, he felt a pang of loss for St Petersburg. He'd looked it up in his mother's old school atlas at home. There was a lake beside St Petersburg, a lake as big as a country. He wondered if there were swans there.

His mother sneered at his taste in music. "A little too obvious for me," she'd said. She'd probably only ever heard *The Nutcracker Suite*. He thought about the atlas again, and tried to place Archangel. Then he remembered. It was in the far north, on the edge of the White Sea. He'd wondered at the time why so many seas were named after colours, when they were all really some variation of blue.

The American woman got up and left the carriage. Adam watched the hem of her dress snake over the soldier's boots. It reminded him of the time he had slipped into the spare bedroom where his mother worked on the wedding dresses. He had poured the fabric onto the floor, feeling its cool slippery smoothness in his hands. He remembered the way it rippled on the dark carpet, the satisfied drape of it, the opalescent glow. The fabric lost its magic once it was cut. He hated to see the way it buckled when the pattern was pinned to it. The finished gowns looked pitiful to him, like the ghosts of ball-gowns.

When he looked up the soldier was staring at him. He had pale blemished skin. Adam thought he looked like a brute. He didn't want that. Not yet.

He looked out the window, and at once he knew how the White Sea would look. It would be as grey as a wet December road, and the thick yellow surf would be tinged with brown where its edges met the water. He would stand on the shores at Archangel and watch half-decayed plastic bags turn lazy somersaults in the dense water.

The soldier took a crushed cigarette packet from his coat pocket. He leaned over to Adam, offering him the packet. Adam shook his head. The soldier held Adam's gaze as he pulled a cigarette from the pack and opened his lips to it. Adam saw the wet insides of his mouth. Once again the soldier held the pack out to him. There was a moment's hesitation. Adam wondered when the American woman would return. Then he reached his hand out to accept the gift, and hoped that he was not too late.

The Coast Road

by Mary-Clare Smith

A girl walked along the coast road. She thought about how it looked as though someone had pulled the plug out of the sea.
  She thought about how it looked like the basin of a sink after you'd washed a really stinkin', dirty mop out in it and the water had drained from the basin leaving lumps of brown and black like the rack and the seaweed she looked down at now. She was pleased with her analogy. She thought about how that was a nice thought, a thought that a child might enjoy and that made her sadder still because it has so little in common with the rest of the stuff that was in her head. She was coming up towards the yellow and red box that housed the coastguards during the summer. It looked funny, so sunshiny in this grey place where the wind howled now. There was that at least, the summer was coming to an end, thank God. Everyone knows that if you've reason to be sad there is nothing worse than being sad in a holiday resort during the height of the summer season. She supposed it was the intransigence, the vitality of an environment created by two-week-at-a-time visitors that posed such a contrast to her lethargic depression. She thought about those visitors with tanned sallow skin who wear bright yellow raincoats. She always thought there was a touch of the smug about these unsuspecting, well-meaning visitors. It was as though their raincoats had a right to their cheerful yellowness because their owners will only be here in this rainy place for a short time, as though they were yellow in an effort to highlight tans that will soon travel back to their natural environment. It was this breed of visitor – the yellow breed, sometimes humped by their backpacks under the tarpaulin, travelling on bikes on country roads as the rain beats down on them that made her wonder. Is that the same rain that falls on her, makes her wet

and miserable, and makes her mascara run and plasters her long black hair to her face, is it the same rain that falls on them?

When it rains you can cry in peace, nobody notices. And when the wind lets rip it mirrors your anger. The elements are welcome friends to loneliness, and a sign that the summer is ending. Her belly is getting fat and she wishes she could make it stop. It will do no good to try to cut down on the crisps this time. She never realised that she had so little control before all this happened, so now she is meticulous about everything that she can direct. She checks and rechecks the locked door of her flat, that the zip of her trousers is up, that she has gone to the toilet before leaving to go anywhere in case she is caught short.

She rounds the corner of the coast road and a woman walking her dog stops to ask her the time. She tells her the time but the dog walker has trouble understanding her accent. She is a foreigner here in what she had naively thought was her own country. She doesn't wear a yellow coat or a tan or even those brown loafer shoes, the emblem of the continental traveller, but the old woman looks at her curiously and she realises that she is an alien in this place.

She is dirty in Holy Galway too. She imagines that a people diluted by the liberalism of Protestantism, her own people, as it were, wouldn't mind too much but here... anyway she knows that she is a foreigner here because she has been to the dole office and they would like to know why she doesn't allow Her Majesty to pay for her idleness.

She walks and walks and walks the sea road as if at the end of it there might be an answer to her problems.

She prays that the baby inside her might die. She has read and re-read the statistics a million times. Pretty good odds, she reckons; 1 in 5, but somehow she just knows that God will not reach in this time with his life-taking hands the way he has done so cruelly before.

She stops to take a seat at the end of this track, having

successfully steered clear of the dog shit, the by-product of the middle class suburbia that surrounds her and to which she is, or imagines she is, such an insult.

She takes a seat on a pile of rocks and looks out to the sea in the wind and the rain, allies to the tears on her face and imagines that she jump, that she go ahead and be done with it. She wishes that she were unselfconscious enough to just lie there, on her side, to fill the forms in the rocks with herself and look out to the sea. But she just sits and stares.

She has walked far enough so that the water before her is deep. It is a different kind of sea from that which she knew from the summers spent in Bundoran. This sea appears to her to lack character. The waves don't thrash, there is no spray, it hides its massive power.

She has sat there so long with her thoughts that it is nearly dark and the rain and the wind have kept the dog-walkers and the powerwalkers with their violent elbow movements inside, leaving her alone on the promenade for as far as she can see. She begins to walk towards the water and sits at the edge of the pathway that circumscribes it. She takes off her boots and starts to climb down the short slope until the water climbs up around her and she is immersed in it to her waist. She starts to swim and wonders how far from the island she will get before she starts to tire. It's nice to have a landmark, a land marked by the industry of civilisation with its diggers and cranes. Just a pity that it wasn't something a little more romantic than a sewage works plant.

Still, it was a lot better than the vastness of a sea that you can't even see. She is a good swimmer, one of the Omagh Otters in her day. She reckons that the island is about six miles out from this point and starts to swim. She does so with determination, believing that she is not one of those people who could just wait around for the sea to deal with her. She would prefer to go through the motions of battling it out. The water is tingly cold so she is soon numb and the sensation is not unpleasant. She treads water at one stage so that she can dispense with the shirt that is slowing her motion and weighing her down. She has swum for about an hour and a half, always front crawl, and sometimes with her face in the water as though she had a purpose and a need for speed. Now, she has started to be tired and the coldness is no longer numbing but painful.

She is still quite a distance from the island and sure that before reaching it she will have lost consciousness to such an extent that she will be easy prey for the sea, even a sea as passive as this, an old man kind of sea. As she swims she tries to focus on the peace that her actions will soon bring her. Above all, it is the loss of control that she regrets, that has made her as sad as she is. People have told her that she will get used to the idea of being a Mummy, that she will find a way to do the things that she needs to do, the travelling, the boozing, the kissing. But human nature is such that it will adapt to any old crap and she is not willing to compromise, such is her confused anger. So she beats on. Every once in a while, she cannot help but allow in thoughts of how this will show the people that hurt her. This will make them think, give them some perspective on how she was feeling, on how they didn't make a big enough effort to understand and even on how That One in the dole office might think twice before being such a bitch to the next girl in a position like hers. But these she knows are angry thoughts that have no place in the night of her death. She must not allow such petty thoughts to compromise the loftiness of her actions, its quiet drama.

She is beginning to think less clearly with every stroke by now and the coldness of the water is making her limbs seize up at times. She is glad of her landmark now; she must only concentrate on the gaudy lights of the shitty island. Eventually she is no longer able to swim and she stops where she is, not far, as she anticipated, from the island.

She treads the water and thinks of her mother teaching her to

The Coast Road

do so. The time will come soon enough when she won't have any more of these memories that make her sad.

I think that this is what happened, they have told me that this is what happened for you see, I was otherwise engaged that evening, in the first stages of drowning. I am She, of course and this is no fiction. With the movement of the tides, a rock had become jammed into the side of a pressurised raw sewage container and as the tide started to turn that evening it wedged an even bigger crack into the container, causing an explosion of raw sewage.

The pressure of the sewage threw me onto the side of the island and after an hour or two I came around. After the swim and my dramatic exit from the water it was not long before I had gathered myself up enough to find a bit of shelter in a storage shed on the island where I slept until I was wakened by plant labourers the next day.

One of them gave me a lift back to my flat and I showered and thought some more.

There is something about having your suicide attempt foiled by an explosion of shit that makes you realise that life is worth living after all. I had something of a resurrection, I believe. In the months since I have found that life can be cruel and life can be unfair but there comes a point at which it stops being like that and that the mist begins to rise, at least for a while. I will never be the same again.

The nasty woman in the dole office who acts as though she is handing me over the contents of her youngest child's money box is countered by the nice lady in the library who keeps me the language books and tapes that she knows I like and are so hard to get. The doctor who made me cry because he knew he could, because he knew my single woman status, that I had no job, has been replaced by the funny doctor who makes me laugh, telling me that all women from the North are nutters. Even the parasite that invaded my body, though he's making me fat, is also good company with his kicks and fists and stretches.

I have found that, a little less like Gloria Gaynor and perhaps a little more like a river rat, I will survive.

The Day He Left

by Julie Harte

My journey as a single parent is still a new one and today had
been difficult.

The girls were more demanding, they were teething again and
I ended the day feeling guilty for being tired and impatient with
them. Perhaps they could sense the pensive atmosphere in the
house.

I missed John. This infuriated me as I had always thought of
myself as a woman who could cope with anything.

I fell into bed exhausted, too tired to sleep and too angry
to cry. The photograph of John taunted me, his smiling face
could almost be laughing at me. The picture had been taken
on our honeymoon in Rome five years ago. The afternoon sun
shadowed his handsome face but illuminated his sensuous azure
eyes. We had everything to look forward to; good jobs and a
stylish house in which to start our married life. Our friends and
families viewed us as the prefect couple. When our twin babies
arrived a year ago, they said we had it all. How easy it is to be
complacent.

"How could you do it to us, John? Four lives ruined," I hissed
angrily at the photograph. He smiled his silent response.

I was devastated. It had been a month since the day he left. I
recalled the morning he went, still trying to come to terms with
the suddenness of it all. He had kissed me before leaving for
work. I was feeding our twin girls, Jade and Rachel.

"What time can we expect you home tonight, John? It would
be nice for your daughters to see you before they go to bed for a
change. They see so little of you these days, they'll be forgetting
what you look like."

He raised his eyebrows and sighed, showing his irritation.

I was irked by the amount of time he was spending at work

these days. Since giving up work to be at home with Jade and Rachel, I missed having adult company and his time with me was more important than ever.

"Be fair, love. You know how it is; I'm under pressure to finalise the Webber contract; another couple of weeks and you'll have my undivided attention. I promise. Maybe we can take a short break away – me and my girls." I listened in silence as he tried to reason with me.

Jade and Rachel giggled as he kissed them. They adored him; enchanted by his easy charm, they always had a smile for their Daddy and both of them could say 'Dada' before rewarding my months of constant love and attention with the precious 'Mama'. John ruffled their curly blonde heads, ignoring their wriggles of protest and then he kissed me, for the last time.

John couldn't fool me as easily these days. I sensed he was relieved to escape the unimpassioned world that I inhabited. After he had left, I cleared the breakfast things and washed and changed the girls. I half-listened to advice on the television about rekindling the ardour if your relationship had grown stale; perhaps it was time for me to take some action to remedy the dampened flames of my marriage.

Dressing myself, I examined my tired reflection in the mirror. I looked like I'd aged five years since giving birth to the twins. My unruly red hair was a mess and I could do with getting in shape. Would it be any wonder if John found me unattractive? All the late nights at work and the recent team-building weekend away were common excuses people made if they were having affairs. I had been suspicious for some time if I was totally honest with myself; perhaps it was time to listen to the alarm bells.

He often mentioned a woman called Angela. She was a Contract Negotiator and they were working together on a software support contract for a major client. I wondered how many of their lunches and dinners had been strictly business-related.

John had recently bought a couple of expensive suits and had taken to wearing aftershave on a daily basis; these changes had happened since our children were born, since I had turned into a frump.

"Need to look the part if you want to get on. Angela says image is important when you're dealing with the top boys at Webber."

Maybe a worn-out mother of twins wasn't part of his image anymore. I decided I would show John that I could be image-conscious as well and rival the stylish Angela.

"Right, girls," I said, more brightly than I felt, "we're going shopping. Mummy is taking herself in hand; new hair, clothes, the works!"

A quick trim and blow-dry improved my hair no end, and then we were looking for a new outfit. I spotted the perfect little black dress. Sophisticated but understated, it was elegant and flattering. Lastly, we went to the supermarket where I bought the ingredients for a special dinner and a decent bottle of wine.

When we got home, I called John at work. His phone extension rang and was eventually answered by Angela.

"Oh, hi, Siobhan. John's in a meeting at the moment; can I give him a message for you?" She sounded bright and confident, the way I did before I left work to have my babies.

"Yes, Angela. Just let him know his dinner will be ready at seven. If he can't make it, can you get him to call me please?" My tone was cool. As I replaced the handset, I felt consumed with jealousy.

She could have been lying to me. He might have been standing next to her, signalling that he was in a meeting to avoid talking to me.

The twins were getting tired and hungry. I fed them and bathed them early. The Chicken Chasseur was in the oven and, once the girls were settled in bed, I went for a shower and got myself ready.

Downstairs, I opened the wine, lit the candles and waited for John. I poured a glass for myself and went to the bay window of our dining room.

"Damn you, John, you could have phoned!" I said aloud. I drained my glass of wine and poured another. Tears were stinging my eyes, streaking the makeup that had been so carefully applied an hour ago. Having made such an effort, I felt disconcerted that he couldn't even bother to phone and give me an excuse for his lateness.

As I picked up the phone to call him, I noticed the car pull up outside. That's when I saw her for the first time. No introduction was necessary; she was beautiful. Her glossy dark hair swung as she walked. Angela managed to look dynamic and feminine at the same time and I envied her. They were walking towards the front door, his arm on her shoulders to steady her; my heart froze. Her voice was instantly recognisable and as I answered the door I sensed she was going to break my heart.

I saw her again a few days later, pushing my babies in their buggy. They appeared to be content with her. I made my way towards her, having discarded the red rose I had been holding. I think John would have been impressed with my appearance that day; for the second time, I had my black dress on.

"Thanks for having them, Angela. I'll take them now. I didn't want the girls to see the coffin like that. Are you coming back for something to eat and drink? You're welcome. John thought a lot of you."

Angela smiled warmly at me.

"I'll run on, if you don't mind. I'll call you in a few days, if that's okay." She patted my arm and was gone. True to her word, we have seen each other a few times since John's death and, ironically, I find her company easy and warm.

The senseless death of my husband occurred as he rushed home for the special meal I was preparing. It was good of her to accompany the police officer when they broke the news of his death. It had been instant; that stretch of road was notorious for accidents.

This morning, the holiday tickets he had promised arrived in the post. He had booked a holiday for his family to Rome, the place of our honeymoon. Once more, I looked at him in the photograph; I held it close, willing the memories of us when we were the perfect couple to come into my head. I don't want to lose the images of our happy times; already the smell of him is fading. The very essence of him has changed from someone that charmed us and made us love him, to a man that leaves us angry, bereft and despairing for leaving us.

I stroke the smooth glass of the photograph until I can feel the rough stubbled cheeks as they were in the late afternoon sun on the day his image was captured on a 35mm film. At last, I feel relief as the tears are allowed to begin washing my pain.

Long Anna River

by Rachael Kelly

"Oh Mary, this London's a wonderful sight…"

"Dad-dy," says Anna. I see her reflection in the rear-view mirror, all hot and bored. We're passing through Dundrum, the castle nestled in verdant oak, bathed in mid-August sunlight, and Harry, catching sight of the mountains up ahead, has burst into song. Normally, I'd shake my head, so mature and condescending, as though in my nine years I've amassed a surpassing wisdom. But it annoys Anna, so I grin widely and join in.

"But there's gangs of them digging for gold in the street…"

"Lu-uke," she says.

Only Anna could give my name two syllables and make it sound as though it had always been so. Funny how I remember that.

It's raining. It usually rains in August; no one really knows why they call it summer. It's just that I remember that other summer with piercing clarity, when the sun was so fierce it seemed to rip glistening thermals from the baking tarmac, and we had a three-mile trek ahead of us through the mountains. There hasn't been a summer like that one since.

Harry and I have hardly spoken since we left Belfast, my mother's lonely, hostile gaze following us to the end of the street, and, in my mind's eye, beyond. *Be careful,* was the last thing she said to me. Harry heard it but pretended not to; I followed the flight of a dark-feathered bird against the louring sky, shading my eyes with my hand so as to look at neither of them. Passing through Dundrum I remember *The Mountains of Mourne* and almost start to hum it, but I catch myself just in time.

"Can I turn the radio on?" I say, to ward off other incidents.

"Of course you can," says Harry, too quickly, too cheerfully. He switches it on and delicate, ethereal Bach fills the car. I half-listen, staring out of the window as the Lough races past in varying shades of grey, then, suddenly, Harry says, "I'm stupid. You don't want to be listening to that."

Before I can speak, he flicks the channel. A generic pop song blasts out. I say nothing.

"Your old dad's been on his own too long," he apologises.

I pull my raincoat on just in case. The wind has a bite in it, though it's not strong, but the air smells of rain. We're miles from anywhere, parked in a glorified lay-by on the very edge of Annalong Valley.

"Is it three miles?" I say, to break the silence.

"Three," says Harry. "That looks like rain."

"Far enough," I say.

"Not too bad. It seemed longer when you were six, I bet."

"I was nine, Dad," I say, as softly as I can. "Anna was six."

Harry's face flashes raw agony. I look away, pretend not to see.

"I know," he says at last. "I meant, the first time I brought you here."

I don't know what to say. I watch the clouds rolling in from the sea, threatening rain.

"You shouldn't have capered about like a loony, then, should you?" says Harry good-naturedly. He's always patient with Anna, though I'm getting ready to strangle her. She's moaned for three miles now: her pack's too heavy, her feet are sore, she's hot, thirsty, tired, she wants to sit down.

"Tell you what," he says. "I'll take your pack if you take mine."

"Dad-dy," she says.

"An-na," he mimics, his tone spot-on. "It'll be dark before we get there. You'll not be able to see Long Anna River."

That gets her attention. She sparks up, all delighted. "What's it called?"

"Long Anna River. Remember I showed you on the map?"

"You didn't say Long Anna River."

*"The map got it the wrong way round. It says Annalong River,
but it's the other way round. It's really called Long Anna River."*
"Short Anna River, more like," I say.
"Lu-uke," she says.

I follow the path down to the river. Harry's cooking sausages;
the scent of fizzling meat follows me like a memory. Anna and I
used to play in this river: we'd wade in up to our waists and take
turns trying to drown each other. *Typical,* Harry would say when
he came down to fetch us for tea. *The only time you pair get along
is when you're trying to kill each other.*
The river hasn't changed. It's as though a pocket of the past
never made it into the present, and Anna's still here, so fiercely I
can hear her voice, the chime of her laughter, and my own voice,
saying, petulantly, *An-na.* I throw a stone into the mercury waters
and it vanishes from sight, with a thick, satisfying *gloop.*
"Tea's ready," calls Harry. And then, "They're a bit well done."

I sleep badly. Maybe it's the silence: I'm not used to the silence,
with only the distant braying of sheep and a sporadic dance of rain
on canvas for company. About midnight, Harry starts to snore and
I prop myself up on an elbow and look at him. All I can see in the
viscous darkness is the rise of his shoulders, dipping sharply to the
pit of his neck and the gentle curve of his head. He's always snored
like this, I suddenly remember: the house used to shake with it
when I was small. It was like a mantra, the sound of safety. When
he left, when they divorced, I spent weeks, months, learning to
sleep in a silent house, learning all the creaks of settling beams and
whispers of pipes. How did I forget that?
I stare at him, trying to remember him, trying to make him *Dad*
again and not just *Harry,* but it's not him; he's a stranger.
In the afternoon, the weather breaks and I wander down to the
river to wash. It's cold, colder than I remember, and I wonder how
we ever managed to submerge our small bodies in the temperate

equivalent of the Volga. The touch of icy water on my bare skin is like an electric shock and I almost leap backwards, giving it up as a bad idea. But then a ripple of light on the surface reminds me of Anna, and I hear a squeal of mischievous giggles, a *plash* of a loose boulder rolled by six-year-old hands from an overhang, the rush of a tidal wave gathering speed towards me...

An-na, I almost say.

But I don't. I half-smile and wade on in. The cold is like a shroud, but it passes. *I remember this.*

Harry's sitting by the tent, staring into space. He snaps back as I walk up from the river, towelling my wet hair as I walk. For a minute I don't understand why he's staring at my chest, then I look down and remember the scar. It's healed well – better than I thought it would – but I forget that he hasn't seen it in ten years. Maybe he forgot it was there. I pull on a t-shirt.

"What's that you've got?" I say, casually.

"Oh," he says, as though, now that it comes to it, he feels stupid. "Just... just a couple of photos. Just a wee album I had. I thought – well, you know. It seemed like the right thing to do."

I don't want him to open the book, but he's already turned the cover. And there she is: Anna, all dark, unruly curls, knotted to her scalp, and no front teeth.

For a long moment, I don't trust myself to speak. Then I say, softly, "I haven't looked at a photo of her in..."

"Ten years," says Harry, more like a sigh. His face is red, his eyes down-turned: my father is trying not to cry. "Look," he says. "Do you remember that one?"

It's Anna and I together, in a rare show of harmony, perched on a rock. I can see it from here – a vast grey slab, dark in the afternoon sun. Anna probably tried to push it into the river as well.

"Ten years," I say, quietly.

"Do you remember trying to get her to pose? She was a devil to get her to stand still."

"It's the last picture ever taken of her," I say. "She was dead that night."

I walk away. I walk down to the river and I don't look back.

"I want to stay, Daddy."
"Well, you stay then. Bye!"
"Dad-dy."
"Bye, Anna," I say. "I'm going in the front."
"No! Daddy! Luke had the front on the way down!"
"But you said you were staying here, Anna-banana."
"Dad-dy."

Flash forward, a howl of brakes, my father's voice, roaring:
"Jesus Christ!"
And Anna, in the front, screaming, "Daddy!"
I can't see her face.

It's dark before Harry comes looking for me. I don't know how I've passed the time, only that the light has drained from the sky and the river is tinted inky black. He sits down beside me. I don't look up.

"I shouldn't have brought the album," he says. I throw pebbles down the shore; the soft clicking as they connect on their way to the water is the only sound.

He sighs. "Ten years."

"Ten years," I whisper.

"She wasn't wearing her seatbelt. How did I miss that?"

We're thirsty after the walk so we stop in Newcastle. Harry orders a pint, and Anna wants some, of course she does: Anna's scared of missing out on anything. I watch with grim amusement as she sucks off the foam and her face wrinkles in disgust...

"You were over the limit," I say. There's a pause, so long that I chance a look at him. I've never seen him look so old. "Your mother told you, then, did she?" he says with difficulty.

"I remember." A beat. "You let me have a sip of your pint."

"And your sister threw a fit until I let her have some too. Remember her face!"

I laugh a little. It's a happy memory, shorn of the hour that followed.

"I miss her every day, son," says Harry slowly. His voice wavers, almost breaks. "Every minute. I thought... maybe if I came back to the river... maybe I could... just..."

"Find her," I say.

"Sounds stupid when you say it out loud."

Sshhh! Anna, you'll wake Daddy...

"Not really," I say. "She's still here."

"Luke! Where are you? Hurry up.

"I know she is," says my father.

A huge splash as she hits the water. She screams with laughter.

I stand up and strip off my t-shirt. He looks at me like I'm mad. "What are you doing?" he says.

"I'm going for a swim," I tell him.

"Now?"

The dark water's like liquid nitrogen, so sharply frigid that it makes me catch my breath. But I wade on in. "Me and Anna used to sneak out to go for a swim when you were asleep," I say. "God, it's cold." He's watching from the shore, but he's grinning now. "Come on, she would have done it."

He kicks off his shoes and wades in fully clothed. He doesn't stop until he's waist deep. "You'd better make sure those are dry before we leave in the morning," I scold.

"Cheeky sod," says my father, splashing water at me. I yowl as it hits my skin – God, it's cold – and I sweep a tidal wave right back at him with my arm. And as he dives under water to catch my legs and drag me under, and I yell with laughter as I moonwalk through the heavy, freezing river to escape, I realise that we'll never be all right. But we might be better.

Angel

by Lesley Richardson

Each night the dog would sit by the side of her bed and watch
her wrestle with the demons in her sleep. He would wait until
he knew the dreams had passed before cocking his head and
returning to his own world. Sometimes he would reach out a
paw and touch her hand, but only if he was sure her sleep was
deep and peaceful. He longed to jump on the bed and push his
body under her arm, just like he used to. But he couldn't risk
disturbing the tranquil rhythm of her breathing. That would be
failing her. He rarely visited more than once a night, but if he
was needed, he would come again.

In the morning she always knew that he had been. His scent
hung in the air and the faint memory of his presence in her dark
dreams instantly released the fear. She never saw him, but she
knew he was there. Somewhere above or behind or beside her.
She wasn't sure where, but she knew he had never left her.

Over time she had come to believe that he was her guardian
angel. She had always believed in angels, and always assumed
that she had one. When she was little she thought it was
probably her grandmother, who had died before she was born,
or a great grandmother, or some faded face from the old family
photo albums. She would spend hours looking through those
albums, searching for a sign. But never once did she feel a
connection, a tingly down her spine or a shot of energy in her
finger as she traced the features of the black and white strangers.

And one day she thought, 'perhaps your angel doesn't come
until you need it', and she carried on with the job of being a
child, forgetting about the business of angels for a little while.
She ran through the fields with the dog whom she loved with
every ounce of her little being. Together they chased butterflies
and lay in the sun and danced in the leaves and rolled in the

snow. She told him her secrets and talked about her dreams. He was her confidante, her playmate, her ally, her protector.

The day she lost him was the day she also lost everything that she knew, everything she believed in, and everyone that she loved. In one brutal second her solid little world was shattered, and no one could fix it. 'I need my angel,' she whispered to the sky. And that night her angel came.

Naturally no one believed her. The godparents who took her in after the tragedy were gentle and kind and loving as far as they could be. But they didn't know how to handle her grief. How could they? How could anyone? Who could not forgive the delusions of an eight-year-old child who had seen her family blown into a thousand bloody pieces with her own eyes? The godparents, the family friends, the doctors, the psychologists, they all listened to her stories of the dog who watched over her with tears in their eyes and an ache in their heart.

But the dog was real, as real as the girl herself, and he saved her life. That day, the day it happened, 'death day' as she came to call it, they had all bundled into the car for a trip to their favourite beach. It was unusual for her father not to work on a Sunday morning, especially then, as he had been busy for a long time working on a sensitive legal case. Normally he would go to the office for a couple of hours to sort out the week ahead while she and her mother made pancakes for brunch. But that morning the dawn brought a beautiful day and her father decided they should have a breakfast picnic on the strand. 'The office will still be there later', he had said. So they ran about the house silly with excitement, collecting rugs, making coffee for the flask, buttering croissants, searching for sunblock and the dog's lead. They laughed and they sang together as they packed the bag while the dog barked and bounced about, chasing his tail and licking their legs.

'Are we all set?' her father said as he clipped in his seat belt. The dog was barking, agitated. 'Wait,' she had shouted, 'his ball. It's in the back garden,' and she leapt out of the car telling the dog to stay in the back seat. The ball was behind the shed. She picked it up and started to run back down the path when something took it from her grip and tossed it into the air. It was a roar, a rush of noise that pushed her to the ground, filled her universe and turned her world into a slow motion nightmare.

The aftermath of the bomb was too awful to speak of. Suffice to say she saw it all. The blood, the debris, the bits of her family scattered across the garden, and the dog's lead, dangling from a telegraph pole. If the dog hadn't come to her that night, the chances are she would never have recovered enough to live the semi normal life that lay ahead of her.

And so the years passed. She grew into a quiet beauty, polite and pleasant to those who knew her, but never letting anyone get close. The kindly godparents tried their best to love the girl and be loved, but though she cared for them, she could not love them back. Her heart was broken and she did not know how it could be healed. She found solace in her studies, soaking up the lives and worlds of other people in her books, and when she left the comfort of the kindly godparents to go to college, she felt nothing but relief. At last she was invisible.

Naturally the dog went with her, soothing her soul each night when the demons would strike. Through time she met a boy who was captivated by the mystery of her manner and fell in love with her. And she almost loved him back. For the first time since death day she allowed her heart to smile, and so it healed a little and she felt slightly free. But the demons still came and the dog still shooed them away. Eventually she found the courage to tell the boy her story and explain about the dog. He held her close as years of tears fell from her eyes, and he loved her all the more.

The dog found it strange at first to see the boy in peaceful sleep beside her, but he knew that she was healing and he would stay until her need for him was gone. And then the baby came.

A little girl whose name was Hope. And the demons found it harder to penetrate her dreams. 'It's alright now,' she whispered to the dog one night when she knew that he was there. 'At last my heart is full. I have something of my own again, something of my blood. I remember how to love. Thank you my friend, my guardian angel.'

And so his job was done. Cocking his head, he turned and padded into the room where the baby sweetly slept. He circled her cot, watching the motion of her tranquil dream, and slowly breathed in her scent. She opened her eyes and looked at him, cooing with delight. 'Be happy sweet Hope,' he said with his eyes, 'love life. And when you need me, I shall come to you.' And as she drifted back into peaceful sleep, he cocked his head and returned to his own world to wait until she called.

The Barefoot Nuns of Barcelona

by Michelle Gallen

They were both very young when they went to Barcelona for their first and last time. They would look back in later years, reflecting on their skin that had been as smooth as sand-washed stone, their marble-bright eyes and their gilt-glossy hair. They could remember their strong bones, powerful teeth and tight muscles. From high up in their favourite places they could sometimes see girls who reminded them of their young selves – confident, taut-limbed girls who easily climbed from the cool shadows of the lower cathedral into the sun-lit spires. Although they were fit and healthy for their age, they were finding those climbs difficult now, for their breath came in shorter puffs, their bones burning hot with pain, their muscles black with cramp.

They had long forgotten what age they were. Younger than the cathedral shell, but older than the stained glass windows. They could remember their very first visit. They came to the cathedral as tourists, exchanging silver Spanish coins for admission into the devotional work-in-progress. They had climbed like insects through the great skeleton of the cathedral, the sea sighing in the distance. It was as though some gentle, giant sea-creature – long extinct – had been stranded and died there, and the sea-softened, sand-scoured skeleton lay on, warmed once more into blood-hot bone by the sun. The stone was just paler than flesh colour underneath their soft fingertips. The walls stretched palely up into an intricate cell-work of ceilings and arches. The filigree of empty windowpanes cast elaborate shadows along silent, empty walkways. They wandered silently, watched by half-finished human and animal figures seemingly swallowed into stone. From time to time as they explored the cathedral, they would exchange small smiles in acknowledgement of this skeletal monument, and their elfin proportions.

The first time they climbed to the spires they dizzied themselves with the light and height of white clouds and blue sky. They stood on a small balcony and gazed at the whole of Barcelona, at the spires that rose even further above them, festooned with ropes and pulleys, with builders hoisting and tipping blue slates, bright metal and dull stone. They stood quietly, knowing that the rest of the city awaited their tourist cash and cameras, and they watched the snake of waiting tourists disintegrate as it flowed into the cathedral.

And on their way down from the sky, they descended the spiral staircase that twisted like a shell. This was an important memory, for they had stopped after a few downward steps and slipped their shoes off and that was when they felt the cool stone soothe their feet. Their tired skin seemed to fuse with the patient, healing stone that eased them into the long descent. The staircase seemed unending, stretching down below and up above in perfect, shell-like protection. They could remember the way they trailed their hands along the round walls – their fingertips brushing the bare stone on both sides of the narrow staircase. Their arms tingled with the friction and they lost sense of time as they stepped down and down and down.

They could remember their shock and disappointment as they reached the bottom of the staircase and the loud American voices from up above, scared, wondering where and when the staircase would end. 'It's very close,' one of them reassured the unseen tourists – though they could not now remember who had spoken. Words were only beginning to breathe for them then – they were only beginning to understand their importance, their power. When they first spoke in the cathedral, they had felt as though they were cursing, their words seeming awful and coarse – shattering the peace of the bone caves. But soon they understood how to use them, so in the end every syllable spoken took on the power and purity of a child's prayer. Uttered words seemed to waft around the cathedral for days after they had been spoken, or sometimes they glistened and trembled like teardrops for mere seconds. So they were careful now, measuring a word's meaning, depth, size, before releasing it into the air.

They could remember the first time they came to the great empty sun-lit hall, and walked towards where the altar would one day be.

'How many years do you think it will be before they finish?' They both paused and reflected.

'More than our lifetime, I think.'

It was in front of that altar space that they realised they did not want to leave this place. They did not remember making an agreement – there was no spoken promise, no verbal contract. They simply left their shoes down and did not return to the safety of their small, sea-front hotel.

In the beginning they flitted in the shadows – hiding from the workmen, eluding the tour guides. But soon they found their presence quietly acknowledged. The workmen were the first to recognise them. In the beginning they treated them as though they were shy deer – pointing out their timid presence to each other without words, using a handclasp, or a slow, deliberate finger to alert their workmates of their presence. Then they began to leave little presents of bread, warm, sticky fruit or cold, glass bottles of water. And later, as they grew in confidence, the workmen began to speak to them in their loud, hot Spanish, which the girls could not understand, but still sometimes blushed to hear.

They slept all over the cathedral, always together, sometimes close to the stars, other times in the cool shadows of the crypt that crept slowly bigger each day. They could remember how their clothes grew old and tattered, how they faded in the sun and heat and water. And they remembered how a reporter from an international newspaper stole a photograph and ran an article that christened them 'The Barefoot Nuns of Barcelona.' Tourists flocked to the cathedral then and the tour guides left them some new clothes – two soft, grey gowns that blended gently with the warm stone of the bone cathedral. Their new drapes let them slip quietly from balcony to spire, crypt to aisle, nave to pew, sometimes evading tourist cameras, sometimes pausing for a camera flash.

They remembered the day the workmen brought the first heavy pieces of jewel-like glass for the filigree of the windows. They watched, half-horrified, half-ecstatic as the glass was slowly fitted into the beautiful, empty spaces of the window, throwing heavy splotches of colour across the floor and through the corridors. They saw a workman drop a huge piece of ruby glass from the top arch of the centre window, and could remember how everyone seemed to freeze and hold their breath in the heartbeats before it hit the stone floor and shattered bloodily. The workmen shouted and argued, swept up the little tinkles into a pile that they then threw into a skip. But for months afterwards they collected the little crimson pieces they found gleaming in corners and cut their feet on the slivers of glass, leaving their own ruby footprints across the floor.

All around them, year after year, the skeleton was slowly dressed. The stained glass windows glowed, statues were painted, carved whorls and loops gilt-embellished. And as they grew older, greyer, paler, and dimmer, the Cathedral warmed with red carpets, burning-bright brass, green and orange and gold mosaics and stark blue and white clad virgins. Until finally, the cathedral filled with hundreds of richly clad men and woman with jewels and gold, who lit thousands of pale, beeswax candles and filled the air with the thick scent of incense. The bright brass reflected the candle flames, and bishops and priests and people flickered in their shining surfaces.

Sitting high up on their balcony, they felt like ghosts and watched in silence as the people below took possession of their temple. Old and tired, paper-thin and transparent, they went quietly to their tallest spire. They stood there for a little while, remembering the young girls who took off their shoes years and years before. They were trembling, joyful in the strong, confident wind that flapped around their pale bodies, the wind that whipped their robes around their thin bones. Later on, in a different place, they could not remember making an agreement, uttering a promise, a verbal contract. They simply slipped hands together and jumped into the fresh, wind that haled them higher than they'd ever been before.

Love Always

by Carmel McQuaid

The truth of the matter was... and there was no escaping it...
she was ashamed of him. And now the relationship was getting
serious, or rather, he was getting serious... she couldn't play him
along much longer. Keen though she was for things to continue
as they were, she was going to have to call it a day, give him his
marching papers. She wouldn't tell him the truth, of course, that
she was ashamed of him.

At first she'd staved off his suggestions that she meet his family
by citing weekend commitments. But these excuses were wearing
thin. Going to his home, which she wouldn't want to do anyway,
would lead him to expect to be invited to hers. That was totally
out of the question because... she was ashamed of him.

He was small, which needn't always be a disadvantage. She
could think of many tall men who had the sex appeal of a
peppermint. But he was thin and weedy to boot. She didn't like
the way he moved... far too fast. His feet were too light. Her
tread was heavier than his. Then there were his teeth... long, like
a dog's or a horse's. His eyeteeth were very prominent. And there
was his personality; it was, well, quaint... but endearing.

She couldn't bring him home. She couldn't do this to the
family. Marrying was a serious business. The biblical: *And
my people shall be your people.* Her sisters would laugh. Her
parents would be dismayed. Relatives at her wedding would
wonder, as she had at the sight of the pretty little thing and the
fat slob on the London Underground, *how could she?* It was
unthinkable. And she had a reputation within the family, and
outside it, for being particular about men. A fortune teller had
even told her she was very hard to please in a man. No. No, she
could never settle for this – or with this.

She would have to give him the push even if it was the last

thing she wanted to do. They really did get on well, she and he. He had other definite advantages, oh yes. Ugly though he was, she found him sexually attractive, close up. He was hairy. She liked hairy men. And there was something Samson-like in his hairiness. The hairs pushed up through the links of his watch strap. His chest was like a doormat. When she looked at his beard she fancied she could see the hairs growing. She remembered a poem she'd learned at school, which compared the Sultan of Byzantium's beard to a forest. His beard too was for all the world like a forest. Kissing a man without a beard is like eating an egg without salt, went the saying. Well, kissing him was a heck more exotic than salt on an egg… except you'd never guess.

And there was his energy. Maybe he was small, and squiffy, and badly on his feet and always in a hurry… but he did have bags of energy. When they stood alongside that energy had flowed into her. It was like having been to Shiatsu massage. She was replenished. He felt like nobody else. And his grip, his hold, his arm round her shoulder, or her waist, was so secure. Unclasp who might. Few pleasures compared with that arm. Zen teaches, if you wash the dishes you wash the dishes. Him… if his arm was round you, heavens, his arm was round you. Was there ever a happier weight?

Yeah, he had lovely hands and arms. They were his only nice public part, his arms and hands. Under the hairs his skin was sallow, the loveliest vellum colour imaginable. In-between colours made carpets pricey but any carpet the colour of his arms deserved the Sultan of Byzantium as a customer. She loved their shape, thin like the rest of him. And the hairless parts of his arm, the skin was so silky. And there was about him too a certain gormlessness. In a way she liked it. It gave her a march over him.

She'd never taken a decision to go out with him. They'd been friendly, if not friends. She didn't drive and one day he'd volunteered to drop her off somewhere. That first time she'd begun to feel uneasy – and had been very careful to keep talking… inanities, anything, all the way. Somehow other lifts followed, until, one summer evening, he had insisted on coming in. Or rather they'd both admitted to being hungry and he's inquired that surely she had a tin of soup in her cupboard.

That evening! Right from the start he seemed to be feasting his eyes on her. And when she'd put on a PVC apron, with a Snoopy display on the front, the effect on him had been as if she'd taken off her clothes.

And so it had chugged along, their relationship. She'd enjoyed his company, too. He'd deferred to her as nobody else did. And they, or rather she, had been discreet. Once, in a public place, she'd been panic-stricken in case they met anyone she knew. Did anybody know? She doubted it. "So-and-so put you in good humour," a colleague who'd transferred his call once remarked. Yes, he's always perked her up.

And now things had got to this pass and she would have to pull the lever. Verbal exchange in his presence was to be avoided. His beard might drive her to change her mind. She would write him a letter. It would be termed enigmatically. "I have taken the head staggers"… perhaps. Or "You're far too nice for me". She'd think of something, something final, that would not allow for any Buts. He'd be confounded, among other things. It would be his Waterloo and what could she do about it?

Only the end of that letter posed no problem. Years ago she'd been told that, in the rubrics of courtship, 'Love Always' meant The Push. It would in this case too. But it would also mean what it said. She would always love him.

May Be

by Alison Bradley

Alfred sits and stares. His cold impregnable gaze falls like
talons upon prey from his exalted top-shelf throne. Creased
lips greeting friend and foe alike under the same malaise of
misanthropy. Dust settles upon his frame like a robe upon
shoulders and, as the rain relentlessly lashed, the cold fragrance
of damp crept from the crevices.

May hung her head and sighed at the stultifying silence,
twisting her wedding ring around an old wizened finger. On
the shelf below Alfred sat a young girl, skin fresh-as-a-daisy,
eyes twinkling like morning dew. Yet the photo pigment had
begun to fade, yellowing slightly at the edges. Now the smile
had faded like the photograph. Slowly, in almost sinful delight,
May fingered the ridges of a vinyl record. It had lain dormant
for years hidden behind Alfred's collection of leather bound
encyclopaedias, their musty odour still dominating the room.
He had loved those books, loved his job, loved to parade his
encyclopaedic knowledge at his tweed-jacket-pipe-smoking-
brandy-fuelled Rotary lunches. May remembered those lunches.
Remembered the corner of many a good restaurant where she
had hidden in the shadow, watching the ladies' pearl-slung necks
hold up Thatcher perms. Alfred usually some distance away. So
distant even in the same room... even in the same marriage. A
flutter danced across her chest. Should she? Could she, even in
the sad irony of her 'living-room'? Even with Alfred watching? A
needle was pressed to vinyl. A crackling banjo melody cautiously
explored the foreign silence. She tilted her head, clasped the
cover to her chest, and swayed with the swish of her skirt
against her calves taking her far, far into the west.

It was in the west that a guilty passion reared its dormant
head and with a snorting trot stepped from the recesses of May's

desires. On this wind of change she unwittingly rode home, home to her range where the deer and the buffalo were soon to raise their heads from their grass-munching habits of village life.

A pair of scarlet lips held up plump, rouged cheeks as they smiled in excited bamboozlement at the flirtatious appellations of the titles that greeted them. The white spines of the novels in the 'Westerns aisle' of the library grinned back at May like polished teeth. Gingerly she stretched out to select a book but her hand could only hover. She paused. The titles were so bold, so daring; they announced promises so alien to her life. Bravery. Excitement. Freedom. Passion? Men in Stetsons or uniforms fighting Indians whilst holding beautiful ladies in their arms against a backdrop of rugged terrain. It all seemed so unbridled, so... free? And the women! Long hair blowing wild and free in the warm desert breeze or tightly curled and piled high upon their head, a stockinged leg swinging from a hitched skirt with faces painted like porcelain dolls. At this she blushed at her own freshly painted complexion. What was she thinking? What would Alfred say? The hovering hand fell silently into the submissive pocket of her mothball anorak. Her heart, which had earlier fluttered in ebullience, now sank to a lethargic throb. May sighed.

"Could recommend this one. Loses his leg though. Bit gory. 'Course if it's more romance you're looking for that one's not bad. I like action meself," said a voice puffing out its checked-shirt-chest.

May stared. It was as if the silliness of her mind was now staring her in the face as the voice took a John Wayne-esque bow-legged swivel towards her, thrusting out a friendly hand. In a farcical twist the denim legs, tucked into slim cowboy boots, exaggerating his egg-shaped torso that bulged slightly at the waist. But beneath the brown suede Stetson and above the grotesque sheriff's badge perched on his lapel, there was a warm fleshy glow May had not seen for a long time. There was a smile.

"The name's Butch - sorry, *Francis,* Francis Biggly. Friends call me Butch... as in Biggly's Butchers on the main street. Francis didn't quite go with the image... bit girly," chuckled the protruding hand.

Had she gone mad? People had pondered that very same question. She had heard the clicking tongues on high heels question her sanity in half sentences. Heard the whispering pews of the hat-and-glove saints on the now very occasional Sunday morning when she ventured to church. Listened to the murmurs of stacked corner shop shelves in folded-arm council.

"Not right..."

"No"

"Not since he -"

Now it had happened. The years of solitude had bowed to insanity. Those ridiculous records and red lipstick at her age! And now look at her in a *public library.* Alfred was right. "No place for women. Don't be silly. Cowboy books! What next? Okay Corral at the ladies' luncheon club?! Ridiculous." He was right. She would close her eyes and bite her lip until it bled then, when she opened them, this 'Butch' would disappear and she would go straight home to Alfred and beg forgiveness for the nonsensical indulgence. She would walk home in the driving rain and the cowboys would gallop off into the sunset, washed away.

But Butch did not disappear. In fact, Butch began to appear quite often. First it was as a gleaming smile looking over the cauliflowers in the grocers. Then again in the car park with a "Good day, little lady" and a lopsided grin. Soon it was every Wednesday at the library followed by a stroll in the park, which was really a sit on the bench feeding ducks owing to his pending hip replacement. But May didn't mind. The sheriff's badge that once seemed so garish now glinted with pride in the autumn sun. His awkward stick-hobbling limp was the suave strut of a proud Mr Wayne who whisked her off her feet, a herd of mustang-cum-ducks fearlessly tamed.

A diminutive figure shuffled around the village PoundSavers giggling softly at the dancing tassels on her new red suede boots, smiling at a poster announcing tonight's charity line dancing competition. *Stand By Your Man* hummed on the wireless. For once Barbara failed to notice. Her electric-blue eyelids were fixed on 'the competition', the 'Dolly Parton perm' in Ellen's Grocers. The pungent mix of firelighters and dog chews filled Barbara's flared nostrils as the parochial ambiance of her shop turned a little colder.

"And two tickets for the dance please," bleated a sheepish voice. Barbara frowned for a pondering moment then with a smirk slid the tickets across the counter. "Two you say? *Oh,*" she sneered, tongue firmly in cheek, before snatching the money.

The church hall buzzed with feet-shuffling-toe-tapping-thigh-slapping-mule-skinner-yahoo-lasso moves. Texas roses flapped over refreshments while rhinestone cowboys tried to look comfortable. May sighed. Alone. A squaw amongst cowboys and no Butch to protect her. Her fantasy of riding pillion was now exposed as delusion. Their stares building her pillory. She looked down at her new red tasselled boots, at her pink fingernails, at her curled hair piled on her head like some grotesque haystack. More Miss Havisham than Ms Parton. A sob grabbed her throat. Her heart thumped her chest in remorseless punishment. Thud. THUD. She scuttled to the exit.

"Leaving? Without me?" came a voice from the shadows.

Her heart stopped. She must be mad. Keep walking. But insanity sounded so blissful, so... like Butch.

The galaxy of May's living room spun with the twinkle of a thousand stars. She slumped onto the threadbare brown settee and let the canter of her heart flutter in her ears. The colours of her mind exploding like fireworks in her eyes. She poured a small gin and, giggling, toasted Alfred's pugnacious pout resentfully glaring up from inside a drawer. And there May died. Looking up at her newly decorated top shelf she breathed her last euphoric breath. A curiously defiant grin danced across her letterbox red lips, a hitched skirt revealing a flirtatious stocking in one last knobbly-knee fling.

Life continued as usual in the village ranch. The cattle returned to their habits of living. Ellen continued to wave to Barbara. Barbara continued to wave to Ellen. Barbara laughed when Ellen's perm went flat. Biggly's Butchers remained open. The local charity shop received a generous donation of authentic leather bound encyclopaedias and a set of frozen lips smiled proudly at the village line-dancing cup perched on the top shelf in a dingy sitting room.

A few days later snow fell in drifts upon the steeples and the spires, resting in small mounds on the shoulders of the living and the gravestones of the dead. A humble bunch of yellow roses lay sleeping on the grave of one May Wilson. The cardboard note already turning soggy, ink beginning to run –

"To my sundance kid

Love -"

The name had already smudged. A gust of biting wind swirled the message dancing up to the heavens, gracefully twisting to the chimes of the icicles, gleefully prancing westwards.

A Philosophy of Love

by JS Ferguson

It has finally happened. A man has declared his love for me.

I am sitting in an airport departure lounge where the same man has just deposited me with my hand luggage and gone to get us some coffee.

I do know this man. Very well, in fact. Though not so well as to be married, engaged or even officially recognised as forming one half of an 'item' with him.

I suppose it's rather romantic. I'm working abroad at the moment and Nick has gallantly offered to see me off.

However, this being Ireland, it is pouring outside and we have both got soaked rushing from the car park to the main terminal. Which is why he's gone to get us hot drinks while I sit wondering whether to fling my arms round his neck when he returns or leg it onto the next departing 747.

All because of a book, which he must have dropped into my hand luggage when I wasn't looking.

I was rummaging for tissues, you see. Desperately trying to shore up what was left of my eye make-up. Except instead of unearthing a pouch of Handy Andies I came across this bulk of daintily wrapped parcel instead.

I opened it immediately – reckoning I could leaf through it till Nick came back – which is how I found the declaration of love on the inside cover.

I snapped it shut as soon as I'd read it. Terrified that Nick might find me reading his words. Because it is all too inconceivable, too heavy-duty and just too bloody corny for me at 2.00pm on a miserable Sunday afternoon stuck in the middle of an airport.

Worse, I suspect my safe and predictable shenanigans with Nick are veering dangerously towards the trashily – and tragically – romantic. You know what I mean. The handsome, successful older man. The younger, somewhat naïve female. An expanse of ocean – or Irish Sea in this case – keeping the two of them apart. And, oh yes, Nick's wife. The beautiful, sophisticated and vibrant antithesis to his fluffy bit of blonde on the side.

Because of course Nick is married.

Perversely, this makes me feel relieved rather than jealous. Which probably explains how I deal with the inscription when he returns with the coffee.

"So," he declares, all open-necked denim shirt, off-white chinos and casual confidence. "I see you found the book."

"Yes," I smile sweetly back, making direct eye contact but giving no indication I've also found the personalised forward.

"Er…" clearing his throat a little theatrically now as I sense nervousness from him for the first time ever. "So, did you…?"

"Find your dedication?" I finish helpfully.

"Yes!" he half laughs, half coughs, waggling his finger at me like I'm one step ahead of him – which I am – while guarded grey eyes flicker between my own steady gaze and an apparently riveting advert for hover mowers to our right.

"But," I laugh a little too, "I don't agree with you."

"You what?" he sounds confused.

"I don't agree with you. I think falling in love is one of the hardest experiences in the world."

"You do?"

"I do."

Silence.

I am becoming a little ratty now, because I am that sort of hot and cold, up and down kind of person. But also because for such an intelligent, articulate, well-educated academic Nick isn't making much sense.

"Ah."

I narrow my eyes, wondering if Nick is deliberately trying to wind me up. But I know he isn't. Rather he's simply a mellow kind of guy in a twenty-year-old childless marriage who doesn't seem to know what he wants.

"Yes," I go on resolutely, "I think falling in love is hard because…"

Two ashen coloured eyes study me and I see bewilderment, suspicion and pain sucked into a whirlpool of dilating pupil.

"… nobody tells you how much it hurts."

He regards me blankly.

Oh god, I sigh inwardly.

"I mean," I stammer on, "nobody ever warns you that while it's a wonderful, comforting, fulfilling – I search wildly for my choicest adjectives – experience to meet someone you can share everything with, without expecting anything in return, what they don't tell you is about the hurt and worry that accompany it."

It has all come out in a rush and I wonder if I've gone too far. Eventually he speaks.

"Er, could we just go back to the bit about expectations?"

And we are off. Not in a Grand National, final furlong, romping home to the finish sort of a way. But in a much more sedate, civilised, albeit inevitable end of the line manner.

All along there has been an unspoken understanding that neither of us is looking for anything more than we have right now; a whole lot of talking and laughter, a shoulder to cry/whinge on when work, family or life are threatening to overwhelm us, and a smattering of the other. Even though I know – because Nick's reputation precedes him – that he would prefer a whacking great dollop of the other.

But I'm not like that. Rich, I know. I'm happy to drink and eat with another woman's husband, indulge in a spot of pedestrian foreplay yet call a halt when it comes to the main event. Still, I think this is why we've managed to stay friends for so long. It's not about sex – he can get that anywhere and anytime he wants. It's about being able to talk to someone about everything and nothing. Nothing for those times when all you need to know is that there is someone who actually cares about how you feel. And everything for those times when I'm paralysed with misery and homesickness, and Nick speaks volumes with his silences.

Only now he's said too much.

Love was never going to be a factor in this relationship. Lust, companionship, fondness, yes; but never love. And I'm trying to tell him this without actually saying it.

I take a deep breath.

"Do you remember the story you once told me about the tortoise and the caterpillar?" His face brightens. Well, he's a biologist, for god's sake. I'm on safe ground with multi-legged centipedes.

"Sure!" he beams. "But..." his brow muscles twitching warningly again, "didn't we have an argument about..."

"Yes," I interrupt hastily. "Yes, we did..."

And I have a mental image of exactly how heated the argument was, unfurling, as it had, in the Butterfly House of our local botanical gardens.

Nick, still struggling to understand why I wouldn't sleep with him, had just regaled me with the tale of a caterpillar who was brilliant at dancing with all one hundred legs. All the forest creatures were captivated every time she danced, but there was one creature who hated watching her dance – the tortoise.

The tortoise, who was jealous, devised a plan to stop the caterpillar dancing: he wrote to her. A cunning, flattering letter which asked her to describe how she danced. Was it leg number 37 she lifted to start her off, or was it leg number 70? Perhaps she moved various legs together? And so on.

On reading the letter the caterpillar wondered what she really did do when dancing. Was it one leg she lifted first, or was it another? As a result of which she never danced again.

"And the point of this story?" I had asked Nick at the time, knowing damn rightly I wasn't going to like it.

"Well," he had studied the unreceptive iciness of my blue eyes, "it's merely an illustration of what can happen when imagination gets strangled by reasoned deliberation."

"So you're saying I'm a tortoise."

"Sophie..." he had interrupted, placatory. But I hadn't finished.

"A repressed, over-analytical, unimaginative reptile instead of the unthinking and carefree nymphomaniac you'd like me to be!"

"Sweetheart..." he had tried again, but I was on a roll. Following which everything had gone downhill; for the rest of that afternoon anyway.

This afternoon will be different.

"Personally," I declare, "I prefer the ending where the caterpillar learns how to fly."

Nick regards me quizzically for a moment then laughs.

I smile up at him in turn. "Thanks for the book, and for bringing me here."

Then I reach up, kiss him chastely on the cheek and gather my hand luggage; it's time to go.

Twenty minutes later I am in the air. The book is sitting on my knee. I open the cover and read his inscription once more:

Have you no idea how easy it would be to fall in love with you?

Read this book and enjoy a rush through the history of philosophy.

And if you think of me, think gentle, happy thoughts.

We both know I will never contact him again. He has given us both a way out. And the ending has been as deliberate, gentle and sensitive as the beginning was unlooked for and spontaneous. Freedom at both ends of the spectrum.

The Sofa Man

by Bernadette Owens

I can't help but believe that things are about to change for me.
The signs are good. On the eighth day of the eighth month, I
moved into my new flat: it has number 88 on the door. It has
sturdy banisters, deep windowsills and more space than I need.
But best of all is the sofa. When the couple who lived here before
told me they'd be leaving it behind, the woman stood in close to
it and stroked it with her fingertips.

"I loved this sofa," she said and I decided, right then, that I
wanted this flat.

It's at the very top of an old house, in an old part of town.
They tell me I'll be at the hub of things, in just a few years. I
hope they're right, because sometimes I can't help feeling as
if I've come to the back of beyond. The streets around me are
grim in the day, and at night, I hear hurried footsteps, and then
nothing. But the house itself is robust, and already full of me.

What bothers me the most is the strange mark that's appeared
on the bedroom ceiling. It's an eye; there's no other name for
it. There's a solid ring around the edge with a smudge in the
middle. The first time I noticed it, I was lying in bed, well past
midnight, wide-awake. I never used to be not able to sleep, but
now I am, and it's part of why I moved here. I'm on my own you
see, for the first time in eight years, and I thought that moving
somewhere else would help. But then this eye appeared, and
each and every night, it was up there, hovering above me, and it
seemed to be getting darker, and bigger.

One afternoon, I stood on the bed to touch it. It wasn't damp,
and it didn't leave a stain on my fingers, and I noticed that, up
close, it looked quite different, not brown so much as mulberry.
Its surface was complex, all disrupted and swollen.

I used to think about it all the time, but not so much now,

since the sofa man. It's funny the way I met him.

One Thursday evening, the phone rang. I thought about it before I picked it up. Few people have my new number.

"Hello," I said.

"Hello," said a voice back. "This is so far so good. Paul speaking." I didn't understand.

"I'm sorry?" I said

"So far so good. You left your number here." The man coughed once; it sounded like he was in the room with me. Then he said,

"Excuse me…is that a Miss Hope?" I was struck by the name and loved the thought of it. I knew I should tell the man he'd misdialled Miss Hope's number, but I couldn't help myself. Mischief ran through my veins, and after a seconds thought, I decided to play along.

"Yes," I said. "That's me."

"You left your number here."

"I did…that's right." I had no idea what his business was, so couldn't add much else. I was waiting for him to give something away.

"Can I help you?" he said.

"Well…that depends," I answered. So he asked me what the problem was.

"Well…it's hard to explain you see." He expected me to say more; I could sense it. But what could I say? I needed more from him. He kept quiet for a moment; it was awkward. Then he spoke.

"Well, there's a number of things I do. If it's structural repairs you need, I might be able to help. But if the frameworks …too far-gone…then there's nothing can be done. A lot of the time though, I can really steady up what's there. Of course, I also do your simple recover."

I couldn't help but like his voice. It was throaty, and secretive, and I let myself get distracted by it. But I was none the wiser, and still didn't know what it was this man did. And all the likely meanings were racing through my head. He spoke again.

"Do you have a sofa, Miss Hope?" And that's when I understood. He was a sofa man.

"Yes. I do," I said, and I turned around to smile at my sofa on the other side of the room.

"Would that be a suite?" he asked me, and he coughed again.

"No," I said "Just a sofa." His question had embarrassed me, so I rattled on, telling him how it was the colour of honey and how I'd like it recovered, and he said he'd be happy to have a look at it. So I gave my address, and made a note in my dairy: *Sofa man – 6.30*, the next Tuesday. I've always liked Tuesdays, and always hated waiting.

I kept myself busy. On the Saturday, I tried to put the room in order. I sorted through boxes of stuff, and decided where it should all go. On the Saturday I moved the furniture around, until it felt right. On the Monday, I sat out some cushions and left a few books lying about. And when the Tuesday came, I left work early and bought some beers, and biscuits; and some crackers for the cheese in the fridge. I decided to wear blue; because I'd remembered reading somewhere how blue helps you communicate.

At 6.31pm, the bell rang and I went to buzz him in. There was that voice again.

"So far so good for Miss Hope." I listened to him coming up the stairs, and when I heard him cough outside, I opened the door. He's very tall, with a bit of a smile, and he was also wearing blue.

When we got to the living room he went straight to the sofa.

"Ahh," he said, and started feeling its fabric, checking its seams, and pushing and prodding with his fist closed, to check its frame.

"It's sturdy enough," he said. "A recover is all you need." I was nervous and offered him a drink. He said coffee would be nice. I said I thought I had some beer, but he said no thanks, since he was driving. I brought in a plate of biscuits, and while he opened his case, and set out some swatches, I checked the street outside. There was a white van parked, with *Sofa So Good* painted on the side. He called me over then to show me some samples he'd chosen.

"I thought plain," he said, "All one colour." I told him I'd prefer that, which is true.

"For a sofa by itself," he said, "the colour's very important." I passed over the samples slowly, and settled on three. There was a dusty grey, a blood red and a moody blue, all soft as fur.

"I can't decide," I said "I like them all." He was standing right beside. He took a few sips, then wandered off a little, with his coffee in his hand. I saw him looking around for a bit from the side of my eye. Then he said maybe I should think about it. I told him that was a good idea, and added that I liked the way they felt. He smiled.

So he left me the samples, and said he'd call me in a week or thereabouts. I asked him for a card, and he apologised for not having any. He'd just started on his own, he said. Then he told me he'd be away for a while, on business, and when he got back, he'd call. I walked to the ground floor with him.

"Goodnight Miss Hope," He said. "Till next time." Then he got into his van, did a u-turn, and drove away.

The next day, I skipped work and took a trip to town. I searched everywhere I could think of, to buy three throws, as close in colour as possible to the dusty grey, the blood red and the moody blue. I fared quite well, and though the textures aren't the same, the colours are close enough. I've tried them all now, for a few days each, to see how they make me feel: and tonight I'm starting over again. The dusty grey says I'm devious; the blood red says the danger is past; and the moody blue says it's good to wait.

I lie here at night now, in the sofa's broad arms, and let myself fall asleep. I keep the TV on, low enough to sound like voices in the next room. Sometimes I think about the eye in the bedroom, with no one to watch; and, once or twice, about the real Miss Hope. And I wonder what to do about my own name. I can't help but believe that things are about to change for me. I'm waiting, for the sofa man to call; he's very near, just eight digits away.

Epistle

by Bernie McGill

It was in November that Monica began to write to her husband.
Not love letters. They weren't lovers; at least not in the way
they had been before they were married. Not in the tangled
sheets in a single bed all day Sunday way. And these weren't
letters exactly. They were more like progress reports. She'd been
feeling – what was the word? Unregarded. He no longer seemed
to know what she needed. Recently, it had occurred to her that
she hadn't told him. She hadn't been able to find the appropriate
avenue of expression. Wedged into a corner of the sofa after a
day of confrontational meetings and long hours of driving, it
seemed unfair to harangue him about *her* problems. She had
gotten into the habit of absenting herself, staring blankly into an
unread page for hours, while she compiled in her head the list of
all the things he'd done wrong since he'd come home.

One morning over coffee in her kitchen, while the children
chased each other around the table legs, her friend Jane
mentioned a book she'd been reading. The book said that men
communicate differently to women, particularly men who work
in business. They live in a world of agenda, memos, minutes
and reports. They are accustomed to dealing with quantifiable,
actionable material. The book suggested that women, who
wished to discuss matters emotional with their partners, ought
to approach them in a business-like manner. They should calmly
summarize the nature of the grievances, outline the content for
discussion and request a meeting suggesting a specified date
and time. They should give an approximation of how long the
discussion was likely to take. They should come to the table
calm and clear-headed, articulate about the issues in hand, and
prepared to negotiate. This was a revelation to Monica. She
demanded to borrow the book and devoured it in one afternoon.

It hadn't occurred to her that men thought in this way. Bill wasn't being neglectful, she realised, he was totally unaware. She had been unfair, expecting him to interpret her feelings through her behaviour. She needed to speak his language.

Monica borrowed several books from the library with titles such as 'Thought Processes in Business', and 'How to Get Your Agenda on the Table'. There were chapters on content, design and process. She learnt the difference between problem-management, and problem-solving techniques. She now understood that she was to focus on key issues; avoid discussion of multiple ideas at once. She was required to renew the books several times. She came to fully appreciate the merit of a business-like approach, but she was unconvinced of her confidence in a face-to-face confrontation. In the end, she decided on a compromise. She would write to her husband. She would divide her letters into columns headed: the action; how it was right or wrong; how it had made her feel. She felt that this satisfied the criteria of the professional method, yet created a safe environment in which to air her concerns. She immediately set to work.

The first day she wrote to Bill, she decided not to include all the things he'd done wrong the previous day. Best to start on a positive note, she thought. So she wrote that it was good to have him home – not early, but not too late. And that she was glad that he had remembered to phone Carl about the meal. But that it wasn't good that the first thing he'd said was, had she paid the oil bill? And he shouldn't have ordered the children to bed five minutes after he'd gotten home, when that was the first they'd seen of him all day. Then there were the things he hadn't done: thanked her for the meal she'd cooked; asked about her day; congratulated her on the wonder of the children; noticed that she'd remembered to put the bin out... she let him know that these things made her feel unappreciated. She finished with a note that she would write to him again tomorrow – about today's performance. And she handed it to him, neatly handwritten on Basildon Bond, after he'd finished his dinner, and had already done several things wrong. She left him to read it, and went upstairs to fold small items of clothing, feeling unburdened. She returned half an hour later; they had their usual cup of tea and hour of television. Neither of them mentioned the letter.

Days passed and Monica got into the swing of the letter writing. She began to look forward to the time she spent with her stationary box. It was becoming more difficult to restrict the list to a few 'wrongs' per day. And besides, she reasoned, she had quite a few years to catch up on. She began to add retrospective 'wrongs' to the list. There was the time she and the children had fallen ill with a stomach bug and the house smelt of vomit for days. Bill was too busy to take any time off work. The following week he flew to Milan on a spur-of-the-moment two-day trip, paid for by a drugs company. Then there was the time, just after Moll was born, when Jane had arranged a theatre trip for Monica as a treat. His meeting ran late and she never made it. There was no point in bottling it all up now, she considered. Not now that she had found the correct means of communication. And there was no doubt that the experiment was having the desired effect. The night after she presented him with her 'Approach to Fathering' document, he came home, picked up the girls, one in either arm, and carried them into the lounge were there was a good ten minutes of tickling. The following Thursday he put the bin out himself. He re-arranged a sales meeting to take Betty to her first swimming lesson. He had begun to come home earlier. His arrival now was greeted with squeaks of delight from the children as they hid behind the curtains and played an impromptu game of hide-and-seek. For the girls, there was lots of attention, lots of cuddles. She had succeeded in energising the participant. They never spoke about the letters.

One morning, not long before Christmas and about a month after the letter writing had begun, Monica was clearing the breakfast table when she found a note beside the cornflakes packet, addressed to her. It was short and undivided into columns. It read "Dear Monica, Thank you for your many letters which I have read with interest, and which have helped me to understand you better. So much so that I can anticipate what tomorrow's report will say, although I should advise you that I will not be here to read it. When you are ready to speak to me, you know where to find me. Bill."

Monica stood with the paper in her hand for what felt like a long time. She was attempting to evaluate. She decided there was a distinct lack of positive energy. The team spirit had entirely evaporated. She put the note back on the table, among the milk jug, the cereal packets, the empty bowls and glasses and the carton of orange juice. She went to the cupboard under the stairs and took out the floor brush, then to the kitchen to fetch the swing bin. She put the bin by the table and swept everything off the table into it. Then she carried the bin upstairs, picked up the books that were lying beside her bed, tore out every page and threw them in on top of the breakfast things. She had some explaining to do. To the children, to the librarian, and to Bill.

Half a Brother

by Korenna Bailie

Killian is a good for nothing. I can see him there, sitting on his 'special' sofa imagining that he is normal and it makes me hate him more. He will never become anything. He will eat bleached white foods like rice boiled in water and baking soda. He will hold onto his smelly hat, the one with the bobble, which looks girly, and bite people that try to take it away.

Most of all, he will ruin my life, and I will be left with nothing and no one.

Killian was born in a shroud of controversy. He was my mother's child – he wasn't my father's. He is only half of me, and not even a proper quarter of this family. My father would look at him, stare at him, as if wanting some kind of genetic confirmation that this child was indeed not his. But Killian's face was bland, with the kind of features that could belongs to anyone – his eyes were a watery shade of blue, his limbs short and curled. My father never failed to be perplexed by the mystery of Killian – my mother would not say who he belonged to. Killian was forever only half ours.

He used to eat all my letters, until I found a safe hiding place for them. Then he would open my books and eat those, instead. I screamed so loudly when I found the penultimate pages of my Terry Pratchett missing that my parents hurriedly put a lock on the *outside* of my bedroom door, one which only I had the key for. Killian merrily turned his attention to the daily newspaper, even the stuff that lined the cat's wicker basket.

But despite this, despite everything, he remains my mother's favourite. She would pick him up and look unfailingly into those watery blue eyes and whisper endearments, as if to a lover. Killian would chortle, as if he actually understood her. I know better. I know that Killian understands very little. He still hasn't distinguished which tap is cold, and which tap will burn him.

'Anna, darling, you know that Killian is special,' my mother would say, when I 'accidentally' left the back door open again, and Killian had been found dragging his hand down the side of the wooden toolshed, picking up splinters. 'He just needs a little extra help from his big sister.'

I know that Killian is exhausting for everyone. I have seen my mother eating lots of chocolate biscuits and the grey shadows are still under her eyes. My father watches lots of late night television – I caught him laughing at Eurotrash recently, and he quickly stopped when he saw me. Meal times are often eaten in silence, except for Killian's little gasps and moans.

A nurse comes out every week to monitor Killian's progress, and a doctor measures his height once a month. She always greets Killian with a solemn 'And how are you, young man?'. Killian gurgles a little at this and smiles in a way that reveals all of his teeth.

Today, Killian is bouncing on the trampoline that my parents recently bought. The doctor said that it would be good for stretching out his limbs, as long as the springs were safely padded and a safety net was erected around it. Killian loves the trampoline, and so do I – but he always gets first go. I watch him from the back kitchen window, and he bounces higher, higher, until I can see his head above the safety net. My mother is washing dishes. The phone rings and I pretend not to hear it. She sighs heavily, dries her hands and answers it. I listen to the conversation, but keep my eyes fixed on Killian.

My mother is sounding quietly panicked. 'You can't come around. You were never to call me here again. Listen, the kids are near, I can't - ' She stopped, and her shoulders were slumped. 'You waived that right to see him, I - ' Whoever it was cut her off again. My mother looks sad. I want to say something to her. I could perhaps finish washing the dishes, which might make her happy. I have to watch Killian though. I look at him. He is happy and unaware. His arms are flopping crazily around, like he's made from India rubber. I can hear his gurgles through the glass.

'Killian!' I yell out the door. 'Don't go too high, you little ratbag!' He gurgles again, and jumps higher.

My mother has hung up. I ask her what's wrong and she says it was nothing, just an old friend. My parents think that I'm stupid, my mother especially. Maybe she's just used to thinking that way about Killian, and she instantly thinks the same about me. But I'm not stupid. I can sense when something is wrong. I am perceptive about even the slightest of Killian's mood changes, such as when he dislikes a certain sound, like the distant crackle of static on a radio station, or when he is in the mood to eat paper.

I know that my mother was just talking to Killian's father. The man who is the reason why Killian will never be a full quarter. A few tears drop from my mother's face as she washes the dishes. I look at her and want to say something but find that I can't. I realise that I have taken my eyes of Killian and I look in time to see him bounce his highest yet. He screams piercingly midair – I see him turn head over heels in the air then he is lying still on the trampoline, as it reverberates. I stand on my tiptoes. I can't see what way he is lying. Killian isn't moving and I open the back door and run out to him.

Do you see what I mean? Never a moment's peace. He is a life time burden, always in trouble, always making me run to him. I have to help Killian and my mother is washing dishes, her tears falling into the sink.

She runs out after me but I reach him first. He is lying in a twisted, wrong shape. His eyes are closed and one of his small legs twitches a little.

"Anna! Don't touch him!" my mother shouts. "I'll call an ambulance!" She runs, and I've never noticed how funny her run is, like a prairie dog, a kind of out-turned scampering. Killian's small face is screwed up a little, like he's about to start bawling. My hand shakes by my side. I want to help him, but am afraid to touch him.

Killian opens his eyes and whimpers a little – it's all nonsense, but I am relieved to hear him speak. The sound of the ambulance siren distresses him, and he makes muffled mewling noises, like kittens I saw once, being put into a coal streaked sack. The paramedics are wearing bright clothes, which I like, but are carrying a stretcher which I know Killian will hate. He starts to cry and they tenderly lift him onto it, and his little crooked legs dangle for a moment over the edge before he is gently taken away.

My mother forgets to lock the house door as we quickly jump into her car. She realises this three miles down the road, and it makes her go even faster.

"Mother," I say, "Who was on the phone earlier?"

She looks instantly irritated. "An old friend, Anna – does it matter? All we need to worry about now is your brother."

"He's only half my brother," I mutter.

"What?"

"Nothing." I can see the ambulance a little bit ahead, and it dips over a hill until it is out of sight. My mother sets her lips in a straight line and turns on the radio. It's an old Led Zeppelin song, *Heartbreaker,* and her lips become even tighter at the words:

One thing I do have on my mind, if you can clarify please do, It's the way you call me by another guy's name when I try to make love to you...

She tries to call my father at work, but can't reach him. We continue driving, and no one speaks, and Killian is still ahead of us.

Life Drawing

by Susan Gordon

She stood in front of the portrait, taking time to search it. It was her, a mirror image only much, much nicer. He knew.

Beth's large brown eyes were shining back at her with innocence. An innocence that was real. She had come through university intact. Foundation year at Art college was a shock, only then did Beth realise how simplistic her life had been up until now, unspoiled. No one had yet found this her endearing quality, as her Mum had once suggested. She had rapidly moved from a curiosity figure to become an easy target. As a knee jerk reaction she had shaved off her long dark curls. Her large brown eyes standing out more than ever, intensifying that look of vulnerability she was so keen to disguise.

Now she was independent. Her hair had grown into a stylish sixties crop. With her first pay cheque she had purchased a car. A twenty five year old Beetle soft top, it had three working gears and only went into fourth if you used your knee to hold it in position. It was draughty and cold all year round, but some day she was going to drive to the edge of a wild Irish beach and watch the sun rise with a man she loved.

He watched her while she stood in front of his work. She reminded him so much of the girl he'd lived with in Berlin during the sixties. He smiled as he remembered how she'd blossomed, after.

Beth turned as she became aware of his eyes smiling at her. Then blushed as she realised how long she had stood without comment. "I had no idea...."she faltered. Now she felt a rising knot of panic, he was more than twice her age. She had enjoyed the flirtation, wanting to catch his eye from the first night at life drawing class. She wanted him to choose her, out of the pack of dribbling desperados that followed him to the pub after class each week.

Sean had asked her to model on the last night of class, knowing he could not yet bear to let go of her image. They had met for the first sitting at her flat, where she would have felt more at ease. Sketching her was as sweet as the act itself and it was addictive. He made excuses to return twice more, even brought his saxophone. She'd laughed as he finished, he looked up, his lips still pursed. "I thought you were supposed to play jazz on a sax!" She hadn't recognised classical.

Beth felt the side of her knee, there was a large bruise developing from holding the gear on the ninety mile drive up North to his studio in Donegal. Sean spoke, "Let's go for a drink," Beth agreed, some air, some food and a change of venue would all be welcome. It was a three mile walk to the nearest pub. Sean had leant his car to his son to pack all his stuff off to Manchester Poly. He was studying fine art but had his father's talent for music also.

"Can we eat first?" Beth was never good at lasting without food. She made her way down to a quiet corner table, where she could take in her new surroundings in peace. The pub was much as she'd imagined, family run, too dark to see the dirt, and by the time you'd walked there wind torn you were more concerned about a good feed of drink washed down with a decent fish supper to notice. Beth plonked her elbows on the table and dipped a finger into the head of her Guinness. She began to feel a little more normal. Sean was chatting loudly with some 'auld' boys who had sat at the bar so long their back sides were moulded into their stools. Sean approached carrying a glass of German white and two ketchup stained menus. Beth lifted her elbows to shift over. As she let go, the table wobbled, spilling Guinness on her faded jeans. "Oh!" she felt her hunger and tiredness return this time with some irritation. She hadn't even stopped to bring a change of clothes. Such a rush, she'd been in, to leave after his phone call inviting her to see the finished work. She imagined how she would mask her discomfort by casually drawing out a cigarette, tapping it on the box and lighting it, taking a long slow draw and then gently releasing..... Never having been a smoker Beth sat back and flicked open the menu. She wished Sean would just put his arm around her. A hug would do just as well as the warm glowing embers of peat that were so obviously missing from the grate in their 'Traditional Irish' pub.

Feeling fortified by her generous serving of fish and chips, Beth felt a little braver, "How many women have you slept with?" "You will be Twenty-six" he answered. Trying to match his confidence Beth continued "Tell me about some of them?" She was impressed by the stories, especially of a girl in Berlin whom she secretly likened herself to. This surely was the man of choice; he would be confident, sensual, show her all there was to discover. She would gather a book of memories to play out in her minds eye. A smile broadened as she lost herself in imagination.

"Taxi for Murray," came a shout across the bar. Sean got up and took her hand. The taxi bumped along the lane back to his studio taking only moments to cover what had seemed such a long walk that afternoon.

He left her in his bedroom. She looked about for a time then realized she should undress. She waited on for a moment, wanting him to see her new nakedness. Eventually the cold forced her under the covers, her feet like blocks of ice and her nose starting to drip.

She woke as he climbed into the bed. Mentally protesting, Beth allowed him to continue, wanting it to become more like the scene in her imagination. Almost as abruptly as he pushed inside her it was over, he rolled away from her. She reached over to call him back anxious to recapture anything, but he had already slipped out of the room.

He had led her to the bedroom and left her. He would give her time to make herself comfortable. Sean walked to his studio and sat watching as the last fingers of sunset gently slid from her portrait. She stood life-size before him glowing warm, red. He undressed. Moving silently down the passageway to the bedroom he barely noticed how cold it had become. He slipped into bed beside her not wanting to wake her, yet she stirred. It was how Nadia had liked it all those years ago in Berlin. For him to enter her from the back while she was sleeping, he could still hear those sweet moans.

Beth woke in the morning unsure how to react. She felt more of a novice now than ever. Perhaps they would have breakfast together. Take a drive to the edge of the sands, spend a lazy Sunday. She got dressed. "Help yourself," Sean passed her in the doorway and nodded towards the kitchen. He left a visible trail of aftershave behind him. He was smartly dressed. Sean noted her gaze and added, "Church and then I have lunch with my daughter." Beth began to bite back tears of frustration at her own foolishness. She opened the kitchen cupboards one after the other searching in vain for something beyond oily rags, jam jars of turps and old tubes of paint. "Would you mind moving your car? Susannah's picking me up at ten?" "No Problem!" Beth replied and lifting her bag slowly she walked out to her car. She reversed out through the narrow gate looking for somewhere to pause and look back. It was a bright, cold morning. Beth watched as her breath misted the screen. As she pressed the side of her knee painfully against the gear stick she determined this would be her last drive in a dysfunctional old car.

Travellers

by Julie Agnew

Caitlin slumped onto the jetty, warm wood rough beneath her legs. Her rucksack slid from her shoulders with a thump. Another hot, sleepy day in Thailand, days jumbled with glimpses of Buddhas and golden palaces. She smiled at Nick as he leant her bag against his and joined her crossed-legged on the jetty. Connor dropped his bag beside theirs, and turned to stare out at the clear waters.

Around her the jetty was filing with others waiting for the ferry. The two party girls they'd been amused by the day before, with their impractical heeled shoes and day old tans, were struggling down the jetty towards them, the wheels of their suitcases catching in the gaps between the planks. Chattering Thais cradling cockerels, their multicoloured tails catching the light, the obligatory Kiwis and Aussies good-naturedly tossing a rugby ball around. Pale skinned westerners blistering in the sun.

She closed her eyes, feeling the breeze hot and sticky on her forehead, counting inwardly to ten. Nothing had changed. Connor still stood ramrod straight staring into nothing, tension etched in his shoulders. Nick touched her arm briefly, and she resisted the urge to slide her head onto his shoulder and howl like a baby. Instead, she picked idly at a splinter in the wood below her and tried to make some sense of what had gone wrong.

It wasn't just the heat and the hangover that was making her miserable. Along with a shag pile carpeted mouth and the beginnings of a headache, there was that awkward, uneasy sensation in her stomach reminding her that this time she really had gone too far. They'd ended up at the wrong end of a vodka and Red Bull fuelled session the previous night, and a drunken stumble up the beach to their hotel had ended up in a full-on, nothing held back argument between Connor and her. It had finished with her screaming at him that she wouldn't go near him again if he paid her, before storming off to sit on the moonlit beach, staring at a million stars. An argument that had been about nothing, but underneath had meant everything. Nick had tried his best, attempting to calm things between his little sister and his best mate. Now none of them could find the words to make last evening go away.

Connor and she had been friends for so long, then one drunken night filled with homesickness at university had slid into kisses. Before she knew what had happened the awkwardness had gone and they were a couple. And it was good. Maybe it was graduating and job hunting, and returning home, but for a while now she'd been worried that they were only a couple because circumstances made it easy. That wasn't what she wanted at all, and she knew if she messed this up, the fallout would be massive.

And now here she was, Caitlin O'Hara, 'a heartbeat away from being Scarlet' her mum would say with a smile. Miles from home, with the people who knew her best. A cat that came with hidden claws. She smiled ruefully. The claws hadn't been so hidden the night before.

A summer spent working in the local pub, and indulging in several sessions there too, left them with money and a desire to get away. A drunken brainstorm had ended with a pin in Thailand. Thoughts of temples, and old railways, and for Caitlin, Leonardo DiCaprio and 'the beach', had made this holiday sound perfect. And it had been up till now.

"Caitlin. Caitlin." Nick dragged her back from her thoughts. "Boat's here!" she followed Nick's finger and shuddered. The boat he was pointing at looked like a floating shipwreck, but the Thais were pushing past them to get onboard quickly. "Come on. Do you want a seat or what?" she was about to make some comment about seats on the Titanic, but Connor and Nick were already half way down the jetty. She sprinted to catch up.

Up close, the boat was even worse than she expected, but the mass of people behind her left her with no option but to climb on board. Ever since she had been small, boats had left her sick and shaking. By the time she sorted herself out, most of the seats had gone. The boys had fought their way to the back and had grabbed the last three seats together. Wedged between the side of the boat and Nick, Connor opposite, she took a deep breath, trying to calm her nerves. "Caitlin. Don't worry. I've worked a way out if it capsizes. I won't let you drown." She looked up into dark brown eyes and her stomach turned over. Connor. "I told your mum I'd make sure you two came back the same way you went out." Before she could reply, he was deep in his book. She smiled at Nick. At least he was talking to her.

The boat began to throb below her, and she stared out at the jetty fading into the distance. The sea sparkled into the clear light, and she rummaged in her bag for her sunglasses, leaning her head against the side of the boat. The boys were now deep in a conversation about rugby, and she let the words wash over her, giving her time to think. If she didn't say something soon, it might be too late to fix what the night before had done.

It was a while before she realised Nick was talking to her. "Drink?" She took the bottle of water and sipped it gratefully. The boat lurched, tipping her forward out of her seat, and practically on top of Connor. He caught her shoulders, easing her back into her spot again. "There are easier ways of getting my attention!" A moment of amusement before the brown eyes were serious again. "Look. I may have been a bit out of order last night," she interrupted him quickly. "No way. Totally my fault. Too much vodka. You know me, drink in, wit out." There was a muffled snort of laughter from Nick. "I said a lot of things I didn't mean, and a shed load more that I should have said when I was sober." The boat lurched again, and she felt her hand clench. Connor reached over and took it in his, smoothing her hand straight. "I told you, everything's going to be fine. Everything". She smiled at him. "You going to single-handedly fight off the sharks then?" He laughed. "No, they'll be so impressed with the flesh on Nick, they'll leave us alone!"

She breathed slowly, collecting her thoughts. Nick was watching two small Thai children playing with a cockerel in the middle of the boat, and she grabbed the chance. "Connor. You aren't just with me because you think you have to be, are you?" She stared at another splinter on the seat below her. Connor caught her chin in one hand and tilted her face to look at his. "No way, Caitlin! No one gets me the way you do. I need you. I love you, every part of you." His fingers tangled in hers. "Long slow kisses in the rain and all." The smile on his face was matched by hers.

The boat had stopped throbbing, and she dragged her eyes away from Connor to glance out the window. The sun glistened on yet another jetty. Nick nudged her. "We made it. No need for Connor's escape route." She grinned back, relaxed for the first time in a long time. It wasn't just the boat stopping that had cured her pitching stomach.

As she climbed out past the party girls perched in their suitcases, and reached for Connor's hand, the thought crossed her mind that sometimes the best bit about taking a journey is reaching the destination.

Trespassing

by Michelle Gallen

It was late summer and they were drunk, their bodies and
tongues loosened by vodka and orange. They were relaxing
in a fug of scented candles and cigarette smoke, lying on the
living room floor, propped up against each other. They talked
their lives out: university; jobs; men; the invalidity of marriage;
the improbability of babies. There was a momentary lull in
the conversation as the last of the daylight drained from the
walls and windows. Then the inevitable truth game began and
trawled its way slowly around the room. Ciara admitted that
she had accidentally run over and killed her little sister's puppy
and never owned up. Linda confessed that she'd once shoplifted
three pairs of tan-coloured tights from Boots for no particular
reason. Claire revealed that she'd once run away from home,
but only made it to the end of the street before running back.
Everyone laughed, drinking lazily, topping up their numbness
with long, slow measures of vodka.

    Then it was Marie's turn to talk. She was bright-eyed with
drink, and spoke quickly and quietly, describing the village she'd
once holidayed in, years ago. She'd gone there with her Mam,
just the two of them. That was before her Mam had married
- Marie could remember her short skirts, her heavy eye make-
up, the way she'd smelled of oil paints and cigarette smoke. She
could remember the way the men in the village patted her on the
head as they stopped to talk and laugh with her Mam, asking if
she'd do their picture. Her Mam had a smile that would sell a
painting even if the customer couldn't see the worth of it.

    The village had been a tiny place, almost engulfed by green
fields that fell away sharply to cliffs. Marie remembered how
she'd wandered through the fields when she was bored of
watching her mother paint. She would climb over tumbling

stone walls and through barbed wire, careful not to snag her clothes, exploring the whin-prickly fields that stretched for miles away from the sea. Each day she wandered further and further from her mother's easel, until she finally came to a small pond cradled in a dip between some hills. Nettles and thistles clung to the muddy edges, trampled into the muck by cattle. She could see no fish or frogs in the stagnant water, so she stood there lobbing stones, listening as they plopped into the scum.

It was then she saw the boys. They were much older than her eight years. They were bigger and carried sturdy sticks. They thrashed at the nettles and whins they passed, slashing at the grass in silence. Marie instinctively shrank behind the bushes nearest the pond. But they caught sight of her and walked towards her without breaking their silence. They stood there, observing her. The older boy spoke first.

"You're trespassin'." He kept his eyes on her as he slowly destroyed some dandelions with a lazy swing of his stick.

"This is our land. Our pond," he asserted. Marie felt a sudden, desperate need for the toilet that made her want to cross her legs and hold herself.

"Trespassers will be prosecuted." He stopped shredding the dandelions and turned his full attention on her. He wasn't much more than thirteen, but seemed as tall as a man.

"D'ye know what that means?" Marie shook her head and he smiled lazily.

"We'll learn ye."

Marie began to shiver as they moved in closer. She could feel her red sandals sink into the cool mud, but she couldn't move. She stood there, pulling at her skirt, trying desperately not to wet herself. Trying not to cry.

He wasn't smiling anymore.

"Take your knickers off." The other boy began to snigger. She didn't move a muscle.

"I told ye I'm goin' te learn ye. Now Take Them Off." She

pulled them to her thighs, where they slid down, then fell into the mud. They were her favourite pair – her good white pants with the heart on them.

"Throw them over here." As she stepped out of her pants, fat tears started to slide down her cheeks. Then she threw them to him, trying to hold down her skirt. They landed just short of his feet. The other boy ran to them and prodded them with his stick, laughing. He hooked them up and flung them at the older boy, who flinched to avoid their touch. They fell into the mud in front of Marie.

The older boy hooked the muddy pants onto his stick, then brought them close to Marie's nose. She wet herself. Hot urine streamed down her legs, soaking her socks and sandals. It seemed to last forever, but finally trickled to a halt, leaving her legs stinging and cold in the breeze. The older boy looked at her with disgust on his face.

"Dirty little bitch. We'll have to prosecute her." He turned to the other boy.

"Hold her".

She didn't run. She didn't even try to. She didn't scream or cry. She'd gone all numb inside. All she knew was that her eyes, nose and legs were miserably wet and cold. The younger boy moved forward and wrenched her hands from her skirt. He twisted her arms behind her back and turned her to face the pond. She could still see the holes in the pond scum from where she'd thrown the stones in. For the first time in her life she realised how small she was, how weak. The older boy was out of sight, but she could hear him, slashing into the nettles around the side of the pond. She heard the suck of his boots in the mud as he walked up behind her.

"We'll learn ye," he said again and then he pulled her skirt up. She kicked and screamed then. She cried. But they were as strong as men and her teeth bit down dully on the work-rough hand that was clamped over her mouth.

He pinned her skirt to her back with one hand and then he began to hit her. Not with the stick she had so feared, but with a whip of nettles. She could hear their whisper as they arced through the air before they struck her skin. She went limp then. She felt tired and didn't see the point in struggling or crying. She felt the burning of the nettles over and over again, while they never spoke. When they let go, she dropped into the urine-soaked mud.

The older boy looked at her.

"That's you learned." He dropped the nettle whip into the mud, then picked up her pants and flung them into the pond. He turned around, grabbed his stick and strode away, the younger boy following. Marie watched as they left. They didn't look back.

She sat there for a long time. The mud cooled and soothed her stinging legs and bum, so she kept pressing herself further and further down into the muck, watching her hopelessly out-of-reach pants sink slowly into the pond scum.

The room had gone almost completely dark. The candles flickered in the breeze from the open window. There was a muted, unsure laughter at the story, then a silence. Marie wished she hadn't spoken. Tracey turned the music up a little, then started flicking through the CDs. Cathy poured a huge drink for herself, spilling a little on the carpet. Someone said sure all men are bastards. Marie felt her stomach heave, so she ran for the bathroom, where she vomited into the cool white of the toilet.

A little later there was a subdued knock at the door.

"Are you alright in there, love?" Marie wiped her eyes and mouth on some peachy toilet roll.

"I'm grand. Just reacquainting myself with my vodka." Some laughter filtered through the door.

"Are ye sure now?"

"Aye. I'll be out in a wee minute." She turned to the mirror and reapplied her lipstick.

What Comes Around

by Pat Griffin

Mrs Paine freewheeled down the hill, swerved out across the main road and cycled along the coast. She parked her bicycle just past the entrance to Campbell's, hopped up onto the sea wall and disappeared over the other side. Twenty feet or so below was a small beach. Mrs Paine skidded down the steep, curving path that led to the sand with ease having made this journey on almost a daily basis for the past fifteen years. A mid-life crisis the neighbours had called it, early menopause even. Losing her marbles. Mrs Paine however, had experienced an immense feeling of freedom.

And Mr Paine? Well, looking back he realised that this had only been the beginning. He had tried to talk to her but she had just stared back at him the way an animal would if it thought you were approaching its food. He thought he might have even heard her growl.

Once on the beach she would slip into the faded, modest bathing suit. She had bought it on a whim in a shop in Edinburgh where she had travelled with the children to attend her aunt's funeral. While the men had gone to the graveside, Mrs Paine had taken the children into the town and bought them ice cream. She should've gone back to her aunt's house and helped her cousins with the food. It had been her first act of rebellion. The swimming costume was on display in the window of a large department store, not the type of shop that she would have ventured into at home and when the family saw the pink and white striped carrier bag they never forgave her. Imagine, they said, she went shopping while we were burying our mother, our aunt, our sister, my wife, our Granny Wilson, the children were even heard to say. It became one of those family stories handed down through the generations.

Mrs Paine would half run, half walk down to the sea. She would splash the water up around her legs and stomach, over her arms and shoulders, her back. However, this was as far as Mrs Paine ventured into the Irish Sea, no further than thigh high. She had never learnt to swim and felt she was too old to learn now. And anyway, she'd be getting out of her depth, in too deep, over her head…no.

Sometimes the kids at Campbell's would come down to watch her. The older boys would make obscene comments about her body that made the younger children giggle and the older girls shiver in recognition. "Well worn," Mrs Campbell always said. "Such a well-worn little lady." Mrs Campbell had white, smooth skin; she kept out of the sun. Mrs Paine didn't care much about the children watching, if a breast fell out, she just tossed it back in. The Campbells had an acute awareness of their good fortune and so offered up their house for the summer months to kids from the city. "Unlucky" kids with dull, pimply skin, gangly, uncoordinated bodies and eyes that rarely made eye contact except when cornered.

The boy sat smoking at the edge of the diving board, his feet dangling aimlessly above the water. He watched the old woman undressing and didn't try to disguise his gaze but it wasn't a hungry gaze. He flicked the butt in the direction of a seagull, got up and made his way unsteadily across the rocks following the sea in towards the beach stopping where the shale, pebbles and stones had been pushed back into a crescent moon around the sand. He began skimming stones, hard, flat pebbles, and greys of all shades, blues, and lilacs, some almost black. One, two, three. One, two, three, four. He counted out to himself the dips in and out of the water. He held his body low, angled back his arm and threw with an exaggerated arc of purpose, the way his sisters father, Raymond, had shown him.

Was he trying to impress the old doll, make her see how good he was at skimming stones? When Mrs Paine reached the sea, she turned her back to him, bending to splash the water around her legs. He skimmed the stones closer but they were almost silent. He was good at this. One clipped the surface near her elbow. One, two, three, four, five, six, seven, eight! Beat eight.

The stone that hit Mrs Paine's skull wasn't a stone that you could pick for skimming. It was rounded, fat, and heavy. It wouldn't be possible for it to skim lightly across the waters surface. It would sink quickly with a dull heavy sound, which it did, the boy threw it in a different way too. He threw it hard, the way you might teach a kid to throw a baseball or a cricket ball, not that he had ever been taught any of those sports. It didn't make much noise when it hit the back of her head. A soft thud, then bounced of her back and into the water. Mrs Paine raised an arm and half turned towards the boy before, with unexpected grace, slowly folded over.

One, two, three, four. One, two. He'd lost it. The body stayed down, face down in the water moving gently with the tide. One, two, three, four, five, six, seven, eight, nine, ten, wow!

The boy scrambled back over the rocks following the body as it was carried out of the safety of the cove. He sat back down on the diving board and took out a cigarette. Mrs Paine, now well out of her depth, in over her head, floated by about 300 yards from the boy's feet.

"I hope you're not smoking down there!" Mrs Campbell was standing at the back door, her hand held shielding her eyes from the morning sun. She was only half scolding for she knew the boy was smoking. The boy stood up and nicked the cigarette, slipping it back into the packet.

"Naw."

"Did you get any breakfast yet?" She couldn't remember his name; it took her a while to get to know them. By the end of the week she'd be like a mother to most of them. "Naw." He broke into a run to get himself up the slope at the beginning of the garden from the rocks and then strolled across the lawn towards the kitchen door.

Mr Paine had walked down to the beach in his work clothes when he found that his tea was not waiting on him nor was there any hot on the stove for him to get a wash. He found his wife's bicycle sitting where she had left it that morning.

He picked up the clothes and tried to roll them into a ball, making sure the underwear was out of sight. What would he say if someone, anyone, said anything to him? How could he explain? Shouldn't he be shouting out? My wife's missing! Has anyone seen an old woman? Shouldn't he be making a commotion? Mr Paine wasn't the kind of man to make a fuss.

He stopped outside Noughtons, his nearest neighbour with a telephone. May answered the door.

"I think Daisy's gone and got herself drowned!" He didn't have to do or say anything much after that. May brought him into the front room and sat him down. Her brother Jack pressed a glass of whiskey into his hand. And that's how it was; everyone else took over, rallied around. A search was organised, the lifeboat was sent out, his daughters were telephoned.

An old woman nearing sixty, missing! It brought the best out in people. Maybe she had just ran off and left him? Leaving her clothes on the beach? A red herring, give her time to get away. Maybe there was another man? At her age? Maybe she'd taken their savings.

"What savings?" scoffed Mrs Anderson from the newsagents. "What savings would the like of those two have?"

What was she doing going down there anyway, the age of her, the cut of her, the shape of her and not even able to swim! Just who exactly did she think she was!

They made him tea and sandwiches, gave him more whiskey, filled him with relief that nothing was expected of him. They fussed around, pussy footed about. He didn't say much except "Thanks, thanks very much, you're very kind," more than he normally offered in the way of conversation.

Two days later Harold Armstrong spotted Mrs Paine's swollen body in the harbour. He guided it in with a yard brush, shouting to Matthew Wilson who was just getting out of his van.

Nearly the whole village attended the funeral in the small Methodist Church. It seemed only fitting that an old woman who drowned at sea should be given a decent send off. Mrs Campbell stood near the back with an anger swirling around in her belly. She felt the beach was tainted now and planned to discuss with her husband the possibility of getting it sealed off, putting up notices "Trespassers will be prosecuted".

The relatives who travelled all the way from Scotland did so with the satisfaction that Mrs Paine had been punished by God in a more than fitting way for her behaviour at Aunt Lucy's funeral.

"What comes around goes around," said her cousin Ida. And they all had agreed, for it was what they were all thinking.

Domestic Education

by Michelle Gallen

Miss McLaughlin trained dogs, roses and us girls.
I remember her best in the old kitchen - in the days before the school got enough funding to gut the room of the leaky old gas cookers and steamy pipes that made our winter cookery lessons so hazy and comforting.

'An awful intelligent woman", my mother would say,
'Not one that should've ended up in a kitchen all her days. She could've done great things, if it hadn't been for her bother.'

Her bother was her nerves. You could see it happening each year as the daylight dwindled and the evenings grew short. The lights in her kitchen would come on earlier and earlier, and she'd be sat at her desk, the life draining out of her until one of her rages would take her. They were always over nothing - stupid things like Tracey McAleer giving everyone five blocks of chocolate for the cake topping, instead of the four prescribed by the recipe, or Ceire Feely slopping a pot of water onto the floor. But her rages would be terrible, her face contorting as her voice rose, her eyes bulging and shining. Her fat face would wobble with fury - even her wart-hair seemed to bristle. We were all scared of those days, but as we progressed from the boiled eggs and beans on toast of first year through to the soufflés and Pavlovas of our fifth year, we began to recognise the signs better. By our final year, we could almost predict when a substitute teacher would be called in until the days got brighter and Miss McLaughlin would come back a little thinner and quieter.

Summer was her season - when she was freed of the school schedule into long days and hot sunshine. She lived alone in the old railway cottage - her father had been the last signal man. Local people had it that he had raged for days when the railway closure was announced, yet had cried as he had given the signal for the last train to depart. And when he died, she lived on there alone, tending the sumptuous rose garden her mother had once cultivated.

'Go on now and visit her. She has none of her own and she's a lonely ould divil.'

Not a bit wonder, I'd think as I reluctantly knocked on her door during the summer months. She never made me welcome - I was always an interruption to a batch of jam or a tray of scones. Her little dog, Fly, would snap and growl at me as she fussed around in the kitchen, hunting out her worst crockery for my obligatory cup of tea. Occasionally she would allow me into the garden. There, among the roses, she bloomed. She could talk for hours about blossoms, cankers and leaves. And you couldn't imagine her rage there, not amid the defunct signals and old railway sleepers, lulled by the hum of the bees.

'She wanted to travel, poor thing. But her father couldn't see past a day trip to Belfast. He got it for free with the train service, y'see.'

I couldn't picture her as a young woman, slender and in control. I couldn't see her ever making that first step, her foot firm on the train. Even though, in her warm little living room, an entire shelf of a brimming bookcase was filled with out-of-date atlases, worn shabby-soft by her fingers.

In first year Miss McLaughlin taught Cookery. As the years progressed and political correctness filtered through even to our isolated area, her subject was renamed almost every year - from Cookery to Food Education to Domestic Education to Domestic Science. In my last year at school, they changed the subject to Food and Health Education, and forced the boys to have lessons too.

Boys and Miss McLaughlin didn't get on. Although the school had always been co-ed, she had never had to deal with the raw energy and scorn of twenty teenage boys. That autumn, she went downhill quicker than usual. In our classes we took care not to antagonise her and tried to protect her from the boys, who seemed to think it was fun to goad her into a rage. But one day Catriona Murphy produced a lumpy batter mix that drove Miss McLaughlin into one of her rages. She threw a cup of boiling water at Catriona. It missed, and knowing that she wasn't herself, none of us reported the incident. We knew that she'd soon be off - that she'd just not come in one morning.

A few days later as we sat in the library, we saw a taxi draw up to the front doors of the school. The Head helped Miss McLaughlin to the car door, spoke a few words to the driver, and then watched them pull away. Unknown to us at the time, the school nurse sat with Anthony Friel in the medical room, stitching an inch-long gash in his arm where Miss McLaughlin's knife had lodged. Soon after, the word went round that was she wasn't to return to the school. Although the priest and the headmaster had convinced the Friels not to take legal action, the parents and the Board of Governors would not hear of having 'that woman' back.

'Ach, go to her, go to her. She's the worst she's been for manys a year.'

I went. The house was dark and cold. She sat in her little living room, the gold lettering on her atlases glinting in the feeble fire. I made her a cup of tea and a buttered the shop-bought scone I'd brought, knowing neither would be up to her high standards. But when I brought them to her, she didn't even look at the tray. Spoke not a word of criticism for the slopped-over tea.

'He's not come back.'

'Sorry?'

'Fly. He's not come back. Been gone two days.'

She sat there trembling, her eyes dull.

'Find him for me.'

I was glad of the excuse to leave. I searched her garden first, then checked the roads before asking around the neighbours. The dog had not been seen. Finally, as the light was fading,

I walked through the fields that backed onto the old railway station, calling for Fly, cautiously checking each thick clump of grass with a long stick. Giving up, I walked towards the back gate that led into Miss McLaughlin's rose garden. It was there I found the dog, staked to the wooden fence with knives. When I pulled out the first knife, I recognised the familiar little stamp – 'Property of St Christopher's High School'.

Miss McLaughlin never taught again. She got an early pension and retired to her cottage and daily Mass. When I returned home during college holidays, my mother didn't let me forget my visits.

'She'll appreciate it more now than ever before. She hardly gets outside the door, but for Mass.'

It was easier now that I could talk of things - college, the books I was reading and especially my travel plans. She once opened the dusty old atlases to trace my route, but they were so out of date that many of the countries had changed names or borders - some had even disappeared entirely. I thought to tell her of the talk about reopening the railway. I thought she'd be pleased. But she looked sadly around her garden, at the roses growing among the sleepers and whispered

'I never did go anywhere. I'd hardly go now.'

I was at a train station in southern Australia when I got the text from my mother.

Miss McLaughlin found dead in her bed. God rest her soul.
Mum x x x

I stood alone in the dusty silence of the small railway station for a few moments, then watched my train pull into the station. From the moment I put my foot on the train and all the way through the hundreds of miles that followed, I never once looked back. I knew that I'd see myself being followed all the way down the tracks.

A Still Life

by Bernie McGill

Jeanie got a job at the photo counter in Quinn's chemist. It was a responsible position. People handed her their memories, sealed in small black cylinder, and she parcelled them up for posterity. She liked to think of herself as a benevolent pawn-broker, holding for safe-keeping and a small deposit, her customers' treasured moments; willing to hand them back fully developed, when they felt ready to retrieve them.

She didn't mind the long hours of standing. After twenty-three years bent over a sewing machine, it was a novelty to be fully vertical. But she did miss the factory. Big Betty Rankin was always up to something. One day, on the way back from the toilet, Betty flicked up the tail of her overalls as she passed Jeanie's machine, and there, strapped around her waist, and over her jeans, were a black lace bra and matching thong – a bulging backwards-walking lingerie model, on Betty's sizable backside! Jeanie's stitching went off the table.

Jeanie had a bag of factory seconds at home – scraps of impossibly fragile material in vibrant, over-loud colours – keepsake from all her good times there. She'd never dream of wearing them of course – she was indisputably a big knickers woman, worn (in accordance with her late mother's prescription) well up round the kidneys to ward off chills. She didn't especially need to work now – the redundancy package had been adequate, the house was her own, and now with her father gone too, she had only herself to keep. But she'd gone into the factory straight from school – and she'd have found it strange at home all day, after all those years.

She didn't see much of the girls now, and she wasn't fond of her new supervisor. Charity (badly named – not a charitable bone in her body, and ten years Jeanie's junior), was training her to operate the new machine. It stood to the side of the counter, a digitalised plastic angel, its moulded white wings stretching wide to welcome generation of photographs. Customers would come in clutching wrinkled prints on old photographic paper. Charity would place the original in the scanner, press make-believe, on-screen buttons, and – in one hour only – conjure up a replica. Charity was smug and professional in her white-buttoned tunic; she kept her 'Black Cherry' lips pressed tight. But when the new prints emerged, crease-free and glossy, Jeanie could sense her suppressed excitement. You'd have thought she'd swallowed and processed the photos herself. Charity wouldn't have lasted long at the factory.

Occasionally, the results from the machine were disappointing: the black less black than before, the white less white, and the creases that had been wrinkles in the original, enlarged into gaps that rendered faces unrecognisable. Jeanie watched the people who came to collect their photographs: she could see that they were attempting to retrieve something; trying to relive a moment in time; trying to immortalize a face they were terrified of forgetting. They would look down and gently thumb the image, the misery of failure, of its not having been made whole again, clear upon their faces. Charity dismissed them with a small wave, and a 'You can only work with what you have'. No one ever complained, but Jeanie felt for them. For these people the new technology was a letdown; what they needed was beyond the machine.

Today, the shop was quiet. Minutes earlier, the dry April morning was cracked open by a sudden, thundering hailstorm. Jeanie and the other staff gathered like children at the shop window to gaze at the perfect spheres of frozen rain as they catapulted off the pavement outside. Now Charity was having her coffee break and had left Jeanie alone at the counter to organise into alphabetical order, the newly processed photographs in the drawer. Jeanie heard a light cough behind her and turned to see a figure examining the machine. She took in the back of a white mackintosh topped with a head of frizzed orange hair. 'Can I help you?' she asked. An aged little face with eyes the colour and texture of melted chocolate looked up at her.

'Is this the machine I've heard tell of – the one that brings the likeness back?' The woman began to root around inside a candy-striped carrier bag. Soon her arm was immersed as far as the shoulder.

'It's a machine that makes copies of photographs,' said Jeanie. 'Do you have one you'd like to copy?' The arm and then a white-gloved hand re-emerged from the bag. The photo was an old black and white, about an inch and a half square. The paper was aged and thin and the image crisscrossed with fine white lines. Seated cross-legged on a bench on a sea-front, were two fine-looking men smiling out across a gap of fifty-odd years. They were both suave in dark suits and white shirts, the one open-necked, the other buttoned down.

'I only want the one,' said the little lady.

'One copy?' confirmed Jeanie, moving past her. This would be her first solo run on the machine. Charity had no faith in her, she knew, but Jeanie was confident. She could manoeuvre a needle around the underwire of a satin basque without stretching the fabric, and she could certainly handle the scanner.

'No, no dear – I only want the one – this one here.' Her head stopped just short of Jeanie's shoulder. She pointed a nylon-gloved finger to the figure in the open-necked shirt. 'That's my Robert. Isn't he lovely? That other boy is Dan James. I want him 'depleted' for he was always an annoyance – awful jealous you know? Just because he hadn't a girl of his own.' Jeanie's expertise didn't extend to 'depleting'. Not yet. She looked around for Charity. 'You mean – crop the photograph?' she said. 'I'm sorry but I haven't learnt to do that yet. If you wait a few moments, I'll get my supervisor. All I can do is reproduce it – copy it, I mean, just as it is.'

'Och dear, I've a car waiting. You can't do away with Dan James?'

'I'm sorry.'

'All right then, I'll have him reproduced too. Only this time – I'll stand up to him. He'll not come with us. Here you go then, dear.'

Jeanie opened her mouth to speak, and then closed it again. She took the photo from her warily, still unsure as to exactly what her customer was expecting. She put it face down on the glass of the scanner, like she'd seen Charity do a dozen times. On the back, in scratchy blue biro was written, 'Robert and Dan James, 1947 or thereabouts'. She keyed in the code and stepped back, almost bumping into the strange little lady who was now at her elbow, staring into the machine. Her cheeks, this close, were scored with tiny broken blood vessels. 'Isn't it wonderful what these mechanicals can do nowadays?' she said. 'Who would have thought I could have my Robert again?'

The machine began to whir. Jeanie couldn't remember if this was usual. A greenish light passed underneath the print; she thought she detected a spark, and then all was again silent. 'It'll be an hour,' Jeanie began, in a voice that she hoped carried no hint of doubt, but the little woman had her back to her now and was staring and smiling into the shop. 'The copy,' repeated Jeanie, 'the other one – it'll be about an hour.'

'Oh never mind about him,' she said, with a high little laugh, and a nudge to no one in particular, 'you can have him yourself if you like.'

Jeanie hid a smile and busied herself with the receipt. She said a silent prayer that the copy would come out as usual. When she looked up to take her details, the woman was nowhere to be seen. She hurried to catch her up, but was just in time to see the white mackintosh disappear up the middle aisle of the shop. In her right hand she still carried her candy-striped bag, but the other hand was resting lightly in her left pocket, the arm bent and the elbow jutting out, as though making room for another. She was looking up towards her left side, and she was smiling and talking. Just before she reached the till, Jeanie saw her gently free her hooked arm, step back a pace, and reach across for a small blue tin of Brylcreme.

Jeanie could tell she wasn't coming back. She was her first satisfied customer. She walked back to the counter where Charity, returned from her break, now stood, her back partially turned towards Jeanie. She was taking great pains to examine the alphabetising of the processed photographs, and ignoring a tall dark-suited man by the counter. He wasn't looking at Charity, though, and he didn't appear to mind waiting. He was gazing over the shelves at Jeanie, eyeing her with wonder, discovering a smile, as she walked back towards him down the aisle.

Betty/Elizabeth

by Pauline McNulty

"If I can just pick this thread through the back – oh shit! It's torn!" Betty's eager fingers relaxed, and she held up the ripped garment. She had just spent almost an hour in a fruitless effort to rescue it. The clothes waiting to be washed lay in a heap on the floor. The potatoes wallowed in a basin of cold muddy water, waiting to be divested of their skins, then boiled to a mush, for she was sure to overcook them. Betty didn't notice that her home was less than perfectly tidy; she really didn't need to, for Walter would be sure to point it out, anyway. He always did. Betty often wondered how she managed to survive until Walter married her – or was it Walter who constantly wondered?

Betty pulled the sewing basket halfway out of the cupboard, and stuffed the garment hastily in, along with the other unfinished pieces of cloth.

"Out of sight, out of mind," she thought, almost closing the cupboard door.

Turning away, she noticed pale rings on the polished surface of the table, evidence for Walter that she spent time drinking tea, doing nothing useful, while he worked his fingers to the –

"Oh, don't even go there," she sighed, and stepped towards the place under the sink where the polish was kept, hitting her knee sharply on the slightly opened – or almost closed – cupboard door.

"Shit."

She said it again.

Sidetracked.

"Elizabeth is easily distracted," appeared on her school reports.

"Must learn to concentrate," was the comment on her piano teacher's report.

Standing irresolutely for a moment, Betty forgot why she was leaving the room, and then remembered that she wasn't. She turned again, this time not seeing the marks on the table, but the potatoes in the sink. Without enthusiasm, she began to tip the murky water down the drain.

Walter drove slowly, methodically. Around him, traffic poured out of the city, people rushing home, beeping horns, revving engines with exasperation, escaping. City centre traffic didn't frustrate him. Crowded restaurants didn't upset him. Awkward clients didn't ruffle his feathers. He never got road rage.

But Betty drove him, well, to distraction.

When they were first married, Betty, nine years his junior, bowed to his superior judgment – on everything. Betty's friends were most unsuitable. They called her Elizabeth, or Liz. He soon discouraged that. He took on the self-appointed task of moulding her, altering her, shaping her. He was skilled at altering, wearing down. He allowed little to please him, and she tried even harder. With a word or a look, a pursing of the lips, he had control. Whip hand. Oh yes, he had that alright.

But something wasn't right. After six years of marriage, Walter was not satisfied. Betty had changed. Far from being the pliable young bride he had taken, Betty no longer deferred to him as she once had. Her former eagerness to discuss, to ask, to comply, had begun to diminish. She had even made decisions without him – more than once. He had acted swiftly to discourage this, but it seemed that a worm of defiance had lodged in her, and the latest incident had left him somewhat shaken. Betty had retaliated, and had indulged in a most unseemly tussle, attempting to pull the belt from him. He had been obliged to punish her even more severely than he intended. In fact she had not spoken to him since.

Betty/Elizabeth finished peeling the potatoes and put them in a saucepan of cold water. What to have with them? Mince? Fish? She giggled. Fish, for a cold fish. Pouring a glass of pineapple juice, she perched on the edge of a stool, hunching her shoulders, hands gripping the glass a little too tightly.

Betty/Elizabeth had been thinking a lot lately. Walter had thought for them both, but lately her own thoughts had begun to squeeze and slither out, whispering at first, now grumbling in ever more strident tones. It had a painful effect on her eyes. It forced them to open.

"How did it get to this?" she wondered. In the beginning she was sure it was her fault. It was always her fault. Six years of being her fault. Last week was definitely her fault, although she would rather blame the pineapple juice.

They never bought pineapple juice, Walter didn't like it. But that afternoon, in the supermarket, in gesture of rebellion, she had reached quickly for the bright yellow carton before she had time to think. That evening, as Walter checked through the groceries as he always did, ticking them off against the receipt, he reeled in horror when he reached the unsanctioned purchase. Retribution was swift, but it didn't go as it often did, with Betty begging to be spared, and Walter magnanimously staying his hand after just a few strikes. Instead, Betty/Elizabeth had screamed and bit and scratched and struggled, forcing him to retreat, disbelief mangled with rage on his face.

Betty/Elizabeth had hidden the pineapple juice. Now, it tasted sweet and smooth on her tongue. It tasted like forbidden fruit, laced with victory.

At the first set of traffic lights past the ring road, Walter allowed himself a moment of reflection, dwelling on his increasing difficulties with Betty. He would have to take a much stronger line – ultimately, perhaps, as drastic an action as he had taken with his first wife. Such a tragic accident. The police were perfectly satisfied.

The engine idled, and Walter flicked on the radio. Swelling music poured forth, and in time to the music he tapped the steering wheel, at the same time listing out loud the shortcomings of his wife. As the music reached a crescendo, he thumped Betty – no – the wheel harder, bellowing his displeasure.

"I deserve better, not Betty!" he thundered, his fists crashing down on the dashboard.

Suddenly aware of the cars waiting alongside, he glanced to his left. Looking directly at him, an amused smile playing about her lips, a sleekly groomed brunette nodded briefly in his direction. Walter stammered a weak smile, and gesticulated towards the dashboard, hoping she would presume that he had been transported by something uplifting and classical.

The lights changed, and she drew away, leaving Walter to fumble with the gears as he stalled the engine. Walter seldom daydreamed, but as he drove on at his usual stately pace, he permitted himself to speculate just a little. A cool elegant wife, a perfectly ordered home, nouvelle cuisine, impressed colleagues... control.

She suddenly moved off the stool. Leaving the glass unwashed, she walked into the hallway and gazed for a long time at the door, picturing him coming home as usual, his eyes darting around for possible punishable offences. She never knew what those might be – what passed his scrutiny one day might not the next. He would never be pleased. The fear that she had been suppressing rose like bile in her throat – she rushed to the bathroom and was painfully sick. Afterwards, she accepted what she knew she must do, and walked heavily and mechanically upstairs.

Opening the wardrobe, she considered what she should take. The clothes, chosen by him, making her older, made her someone else. Pulling them from the hangers, she flung them around the room, ripping and tearing. Tears of anger at herself stung her cheeks.

Hysterical, she toppled furniture, spilt shampoo and aftershave, scattered talcum powder. Then, trembling with reverberating stress, she stopped. Calmly she walked downstairs, not at all distracted. Going to his desk, she found the key he had fancied she was too stupid to discover. He always closed the study door while he counted out the grocery money he gave her; so she knew it was in there somewhere.

Glancing at her watch, Elizabeth/Betty knew she must hurry. Just minutes later she found it.

Quickly grabbing as much as she could cram into her shoulder bag, she stumbled from the room, a trail of notes fluttering along behind her. Into the kitchen, she lifted the carton of pineapple juice, then walked deliberately upstairs again, her heart becoming lighter at every step.

She hummed a little as she heaped his expensive suits on the bed, then slowly and pleasurably drizzled the rest of the pineapple juice over them.

Leaving the door swinging gently open, Elizabeth left.

The last traffic lights before turning off the main road were just ahead when Walter noticed the brunette again. His heart gave a little pleasure skip, and he decided to draw level, perhaps catch her eye again. She was a little ahead, so he accelerated rather more quickly that he intended. Witnesses agreed there was nothing the driver of the oil tanker could have done to avoid him.

Walter was easily distracted.

Biting the Bullet

by Aideen D'Arcy

"Why," I asked her, "are you carrying a spent bullet in your purse?"

She peered at me over the top of her glasses, the ones she had sat on and mended with insulating tape.

"Do you not remember the night the policeman was shot outside our door?"

Of course I remembered. Early evening, early spring, 1981. We were in the basement kitchen of our soon-to-be-condemned Edwardian terrace, when we heard a loud bang from the front street. It wasn't an explosion. That wouldn't have brought us running up the stairs to street level to investigate. This was a road traffic accident, two cars, minor injuries, disputed responsibility. We lost interest.

"I'll just run over to the shop while I'm here," she said. My mother loved a run to the shop; it was the highlight of her day.

We stood for a moment chatting to a neighbour, till a burst of gunfire from the roof of the empty warehouse sent us diving indoors for cover, hitting the floor. We waited. There was an answering salvo from the patrol that a moment before had been interviewing two angry young drivers, then another blast from the roof. We lay tense, inert, and then the sound of running feet brought us both upright. My mother fell through the open doorway, white wet look raincoat flapping, face wan. My father dragged her into the room, onto the floor.

"For Christ's sake! Don't you know that was gunfire?" She was indignant.

"But you two were standing at the door!"

"That's no reason for you to get killed;

"You might have known we'd take cover."

We were interrupted by another volley, convincing us that the best place to be was in the basement. We waited for a chance to creep downstairs, correctly guessing there would be a lull before the next exchange, like counting the seconds between lightning flash and thunder brattle, to estimate how far away the storm is. We resumed our defensive positions in the kitchen, switching off the lights so as not to provide anyone with a focal point. My aunt refused to leave her chair by the fire where she continued to knit, arguing that if the shooting was at the front of the house, we were perfectly safe in the back. This logic didn't appeal much to me so I remained on the floor. My mother threw a disparaging glance at her sister.

"Madame Defarge," she mouthed at me. My fit of the giggles was swiftly curtailed by the sound of another footstep in our hallway. We glared at each other. Had nobody remembered to shut the front door? No one had. There was a scuffle, a thump, and then a voice, an agitated and frightened voice, into which the owner was endeavouring to inject a note of authority.

"Police here. Don't move, stay calm, and keep your heads down."

My mother and I exchanged looks. What did he expect us to do? Dance? My father, with rather more courtesy, assured him that we would.

"Have you any women down there?"

"Three," answered my dad.

"Youse'll be all right, dears," assured our Robin Hood. "We've got reinforcements, and the big man's on his way."

"Who the hell is the big man?" demanded my mother. Did I hear right?

"He means the army," replied my dad. Briefly I knew how he knew.

"Don't be afraid, now," resumed our man in the hall. "I'm going to shoot out this streetlight, so there will be a bit of a noise, but youse'll be fine."

Our house always had the dubious honour of having a street

light on or near it. In the days of gas lighting, the lamp standard was opposite the front door, but sometime in my childhood electricity arrived, and now a fluorescent appendage occupied the space between the two top windows, about ten feet of the ground. It was this facility that our man now attempted to decommission. There followed about fifteen minutes of the sublimest farce, for such was his state of object terror that try as he might he could not hit that light. He was armed with a revolver and a Sten gun, and he emptied both of these at least twice without success. I felt sorry for him. Any kid in our street could have knocked it out with a catapult. I myself, at seventeen, could have bashed it to bits with the head of a brush, but the flower of manhood grovelling in our doorway saw success elude him.

It can't have helped when it occurred to him that someone might mistake him for the enemy. His attempts to disable the illumination became punctuated with cries of,

"Don't shoot me! I'm in this doorway! Has the big man come yet?"

"Surely he shouldn't be shouting like that? He'll only draw attention to himself." I was no military tactician, but it occurred to me that in his position I'd be keeping mighty quite. My dad agreed.

"The only thing is," he ventured, "I'd say whoever started the shooting has scarpered by now. Have you noticed that all the gunfire is coming from the side of the street?"

"Most of it from our front hall," put in my aunt. Another scuffle, and again the voice.

"Sir? Do you think I could have a drink of water?"

"Don't you dare go up those stairs!" shrieked my mother.

"But you couldn't refuse a man a glass of water..."

"If he gets shot," remarked my aunt, who was notoriously house-proud, "there will be an awful lot of blood to clear up."

In the ensuing silence, my father crawled upstairs with the

water. He came back with news.

"There's one policeman wounded." Then:

"Hello? I'm going to have another go at that light."

"Sweet Jesus," said my mother, "He'll probably shoot himself and us as well, for he'll never hit that thing in a million years."

The long night wore away, the grey dawn saw us sitting up drinking tea and the fusillade ended. The streetlight shone defiantly through it all, and remained illuminated throughout the next day. Our resident marksman had one final communication for us.

"I've collected the cartridges, but there might be one or two lying in your hall. Maybe you'd gather them up and hand them into the barracks tomorrow."

Then he was gone.

My mother snorted. "Gather them up, surely," she said, "but he needn't think I'm going into the barracks with a bag of bullets. If I was seen..."

Next day, every house on the road was searched except ours. We had a visit from a police inspector and a constable, who, when my mother opened the door, greeted her with,

"So this is number 25!"

My mother smiled at them in that way she had.

"Yes," she said sweetly. "One of your officers took shelter in our hall last night, and he asked me to return these to the station." She indicated the several hundred cartridges we had recovered.

"I'll take them," the inspector offered. "It'll save you a walk."

Two days later, she found one solitary cartridge lodged in a flower pot.

"Why have you kept it all these years?" I wanted to know.

"Well I wasn't going to walk up to the police station with one bullet case. I was afraid to put it in the bin in case they came back to search the houses and thought I was withholding evidence, so I stuck it in my purse for the time being, and now

I'm quite attached to it."

I took it out and tossed it over to her. She caught it deftly, throwing it from one hand to the other and back again. She sighed.

"That young policeman died, you know," she said, "and I'm ashamed to say I don't even remember his name. I remember that Mrs. Devlin gave him first aid, and Charlie McKinley drove him to hospital in case they stopped the ambulance coming up the road."

I nodded. "I know. And the following week his family put a notice in the paper thanking the neighbours for all the help they had given, and the condolences they sent. God, what a night. And you could have been killed too. You were always an idiot."

She grinned. "Not as big an idiot as that craythur that was clockin' in our front hall – our bit of light relief, eh?"

I grimaced.

"But why are you keeping this thing now?"

She flipped it over to me and I automatically put it back among her loose change and rosary beads.

"I'm going to write a book about it."

"Oh aye, right."

"No, seriously, I even have a title for it,"

"Go on then."

"*Comedy, Tragedy, and Farce: a Tripartite History of Ireland.*"

"It'll be a best-seller," I said.

The Calling

by Katherine Caulfield

The summer I left university, the weather mocked me in its intensity. Periods of blazing heat were torn apart by tremendous thunderstorms, while I blew along in a lazy breeze, meandering and without direction. I had dropped out of Uni without graduating, bored of its routine and fearful I was being swept towards an unfulfilling career in middle management. I imagined that if I was free and available, someone would take a shine to me in a bar some day and offer me a more gainful employment, though I hadn't even thought about what that might be.

I had moved into a room in a shared flat down town in a street that was neither run-down nor particularly pleasing to the eye. The room was bright and sparse, facing onto a gravel parking area where spinning tyres sent stones spattering across my window at all hours of the day and night. I fell in with a crowd of other young men who worked in the day and drank through each of the sweaty, damp nights. They were a curious mixture of people, most of whom had worked ever since leaving school, early and with few qualifications. Added to these were a few from moneyed backgrounds who ran hand-me-down businesses they had no interest in, all equally dissatisfied and disillusioned and to my mind, incredibly fun. I enjoyed playing the hero I became in their eyes, having shunned the 'easy option', as we saw it, and given myself over to a more worthy reflection on life.

After the first few months of my new life, however, I had become entirely immersed in their routine. Scattered around the town as we were, we would meet at the start of every evening in the same bar before moving on to storm the streets until dawn. On the days when I wasn't working odd jobs, which happened more and more as time went on, I began to spend most of my time there, drinking and thinking on my own before my new friends arrived at nightfall.

The sign above the door of the establishment read 'Sunshine Beachwear', a legacy from the owner's ex-wife, who, while married to him, had kept a shop on the premises. She had left several years ago when he began to complain about her long-standing affair with the company accountant. The sign, however, had stayed. Now, the bar remained makeshift and itinerant looking, attracting and repelling in equal measures a clientele of drunks and homeless. All were too out of it to mind the owner, who took advantage of the drunks and the mentals and sat at the bar all day, a greasy slab of meat, hoking winkles with a Kirby grip from a dirty bucket.

The only waitress was a distant cousin of the owner. She was small and thin and drifted around the bar entirely unperturbed by the strangeness of the people. Her name was Isabella, but the first day I saw her, she was wearing a name badge that read 'Kitsy' in square red letters. I probably wouldn't have noticed, but for the fact that it read 'Cindy' the next day, and 'Judy' the day after that.

"I lost my badge," she explained. "So-o, Maurice there just makes up names because there's none of the right letters left. It doesn't bother me. I mean, not really."

No matter what name she wore, Maurice was never off her back throughout the day. He swore at her continually, berating her for pandering to customers who didn't spend any money, or for forgetting to charge for the gristly soup, the only food served in the place, which I discovered she gave away secretly to hungry drunks and homeless who came to the back door.

One stormy, humid day, I was sharing a table with an entertaining lady who kept me amused with stories from her time as a countess in Russia.

"Miss," she called out, "Can I have somethenk to wash my hends?"

The girl pointed towards the toilet at the end of the bar.

"No, no," the lady said with her heavy foreign accent, "I cannot. My het is attached to my leg." With this, she swivelled round to show a wide brimmed hat tied to her leg with ribbon. "Jou see?" Clearly, no further explanation was coming. The girl raised one eyebrow at me and shrugged. She filled a basin with water at the bar, and brought it to the lady with paper towels to dry her hands. The owner walked past and stared in disbelief at the scene.

"What the hell is going on here? What is this - a beauty parlour? Some sort of nuthouse, maybe? Listen, how many times? We sell food and drink, anything else they want is not your problem, you got that? You think you're Florence effing Nightingale or something, wha'?. Jeez us."

When he ranted like this, the girl would stare blankly at a spot somewhere beyond his left shoulder. I could tell he thought she wasn't all there, more than just dizzy or slightly forgetful. Certainly, when he was shouting at her, the staring, glazed look her eyes took on as she gazed in to space did her no favours. Often, the words 'thick' and 'stupid' and even 'bitch' would drift towards me through the smoky air. But I knew from the conversations we'd had as I sat in the bar, getting drunk and pitying those trudging along the nine-to five road to the retirement home, that she was intelligent and insightful, for all her abstraction.

I asked her one day: "What are you doing working here? You don't have to take this, you know?

She shrugged crookedly in the way she always did, her left shoulder coming up higher than the other. "It's not so bad."

"Not so bad? You're not planning on staying here, are you?

"Most likely. Can't think where else I would go, to be honest."

"What do you mean? There's plenty of places you could go! You're only – how old are you anyway?"

"Sixteen," she whispered

"Sixteen. Jeez us." It shocked me, and took the wind out of my sails for a second. She looked older, for all her smallness. "You're only sixteen for flip sake, isn't there anything you want to do?" I was on a roll again, but she interrupted.

"Do you want to see something?"

Without waiting for a response, she ducked behind the bar and emerged carrying a white bucket. I followed her through the door and into the street. Dipping her hand in to the bucket she closed her fingers around whatever was inside.

"Are you ready?"

I nodded.

She removed her fist from the bucket and threw a hundred pieces of dry bread and crusts of sandwiches and heels of loaves into the air. Not one piece ever reached the ground, as suddenly, the air was filled with birds snatching and squabbling over the feast. Her face beamed and she breathed a laugh as she watched the fluttering shapes dive and swoop with a clatter of wings before soaring back upwards.

"There," she said, smiling and turning to me when the last beat of wings had died away, "That's what I want. Just that."

I just stared at her, standing there with birds tumbling around her, not comprehending.

At my blank face her smile vanished. "Well, what does it matter to you anyway? Who are you to ask me what I'm going to do with my life? You spend your whole time feeling sorry for everyone else, but what the hell are you doing that's so special anyway? Nothing, that's what! No-thing!"

Her words hit me hard, a bony fist in the stomach as the last beat of wings died away with the echo of her voice in the empty street.

I left the town for good later that day, carrying my things in two plastic bags. But before I got on the bus to god knows where, I found myself wandering back to the bar. I wanted to

tell her that I was going, that I was going to do something – I
still didn't know what, but definitely something. When I got
there, big Maurice was wearing an apron and serving beers to a
table of underage Indian boys. He told me Isabella had gone, he
didn't know where, but he was going to skin her when she got
back – "Jeez us."

I found a job shortly after, nothing special, but I made some
friends and I would go for walks and sometimes rent a boat to
go sailing round the harbour at the weekend. I would think a
lot about Isabella, working in that bar with the weirdoes and
drunks and that grouchy boss, with the faded sign hanging sadly
above the door, and I would try to understand her. I could only
hope she had never gone back, but somehow, I feel sure that
she got what she wanted. And every now and then, in the cool
evening at the end of another mild, calm day, I can hear the flap
and crack of birds' wings, and I realise that, in some strange
way, so have I.

Words of Wisdom

by Tammy Moore

Jilly sat on the toilet with her knickers around her knees and stared at the graffiti on the cubicle wall. Reading messages inked into the door was the only thing stopping her dissolving into tears. She would start at the top and work her way down the wall, gritting her teeth and starting against whenever she realised that she wasn't reading the writing just staring at it through a wash of tears.

So far she had reached the lock three times.

"I thought you'd have seen the writing on the wall," Kevin had said. "That's your thing after all."

Tomorrow night he would repeat his witticism to his friends and they would all share a good laugh at her expense.

Jilly had sat there, hot and breathless, feeling like everyone in the Empire was looking at her. When the waitress came over to check that the food was alright she had scrambled to her feet, excused herself vaguely and ran out of the room to get to the toilets. Then she had locked herself in a stall and down to try and compose herself.

It wasn't working too well. Despite her best efforts, Jilly felt her eyes filling with tears and she tore a sheet and a half of toilet paper off the roll. She pulled a face, upper lip tucked around her teeth and eyes exaggeratedly wide, and dabbed tears from the tender skin under her eyes. Then she blew her nose on the mascara stained paper and dropped it between her legs into the toilet bowl.

Sniffing miserably she stared at the door.

'Men are BASTARDS,' someone had scratched on the door. Anger making the letters jagged and driving the point of whatever had been used, the point of a metal nail file or a key perhaps, deep into the white Formica that covered the door.

It felt like someone was commiserating with her and she certainly agreed with the sentiment.

Tonight was meant to be about her. It had taken three years from conception to finished product to get her book published. Now in a month *Writing on the Wall: Wit and Wisdom from the Toilet Stall* was going on sale. So, of course, Kevin picked tonight to tell her that it was over. No wonder, she thought, that he wanted to go for a cheap pizza at the Empire instead of somewhere more expensive. Why waste his money?

When had he turned into such a dick? Jilly shook her head, carefully curled red hair brushing her shoulder, and snorted softly. No, he'd always been a dick. She'd just always made excuses for him before. When he picked her birthday to announce that he had been given important case at work, he'd just been excited. And he hadn't understood how important getting her publishing deal was to her.

"After all it's not real writing," he'd point out, "just stuff some vandal wrote on a loo."

So he hadn't meant to upset her when he'd hijacked that party to tell everyone about his expensive new car.

"Hey!" Someone in a, Jilly glanced down, blue pair of Doc Martens banged on the toilet door hard enough to nearly rattle the simple lock free. "Did you fall down the bog in there, or what?"

"Piss off!" Jilly yelled, giving the door a kick for emphasis. It wasn't like her to swear. She didn't have the knack for it; her voice wobbled and part of the off seemed to come down her nose. However, Ms Blue DMs seemed convinced to give up and wait for another toilet with only a muttered 'bitch' in parting.

Jilly's angry scowl crumpled miserably and she let her head drop until her chin touched her chest. The position let her look straight through the vee of her parted thighs into the toilet bowl. She lifted her head. Miserable though she was her mood could not be maintained while looking at a used tissue floating in a lake of pee.

'I think U R hot,' announced someone in tiny, red lettering from just below the hinge of the door.

Jilly smiled a little, flattered despite knowing that the person who had wrote the missive had never seen her. But that was the whole point of her book, after all. That was the theory that made it more than 'stuff some vandal wrote on a loo'.

The ladies loos in any country in the world, Jilly claimed in her book, were a primitive blog. They were an expression of the subconscious group mind, a community linked by sisterhood. (Not that she had actually examined toilet doors from around the world. Her research had been limited to Great Britain and a holiday to Florida where she had been disappointed at the pristine state of the loos in Disney.)

It was something Jilly had believed for years. She had always felt that the slogans scratched into doors and desks were, somehow, messages directed just to her. Although she had never told anyone she had made most of the most important decisions in her life in public toilets.

'Call Dale on 0141 564 6698 for a good time!' had determined that she would tell UCAS she was going to go to Glasgow University to study English.

'I *heart* Jamie.' 'No you don't' 'Shut up!' 'U know she's right,' was the brisk conversation on the wall of the second floor toilet in the English department in Glasgow that made her decide to end her relationship with her fiancé Bobby.

And when she was contemplating moving back home to Belfast, the wistful note in the ammonia-stinking train toilets that 'there's no place like home' was the final push to convince her it was the right idea.

Moving in with Kevin was the only time the method had let her down.

When the thought of Kevin resurfaced in her mind, Jilly sucked in a ragged breath like she'd been punched in the gut.

'What do you call a bus of lawyers at the bottom of the sea?' Some wag had strayed onto the wall of the stall to ask. 'A good start,' someone had answered below in a different coloured pen.

Kevin was an accountant instead of a lawyer but the thought of him at the bottom of the sea was still a pleasant one right now. He could hang out with the five years of her life he had just flushed down the drain.

That pricked the nascent bubble of anger and Jilly started sniffing pathetically again. She ripped a handful of tissue from the roll and pressed it against her nose. She had to stop this. No matter how bad she felt she couldn't stay in the toilet all night but, what was she to do next?

The thought of going back into the bar made her feel sick and she doubled over. Everyone would be looking at her, they'd all know that she'd had a fight with Kevin, and she'd have to speak to him. Knowing Kevin he would want to talk about 'dissolving their relationship' like it was a business deal gone wrong.

They would have to do it eventually, of course. Work out who kept the flat and who moved out, who owned the Intermission DVD and who got custody of their friends. But she wasn't up to that tonight.

'ROSES ARE RED, VIOLETS ARE BLUE,' the verse shouted from the top of the door. The letters were different colours, blue, red, green and black like those four in one pens Jilly had loved in school. 'WHEN I LOOK AT YOU, I WANT TO SPEW.'

The judgement made Jilly hunch her shoulders miserably. She had never been brave. Conflict made her wilt like a dehydrated petunia. It wasn't something she could change. No matter what anyone said she just couldn't go back into the bar to face Kevin. The problem was that her coat was in there and her purse, with her keys and her money in it.

She rubbed her finger under her nose, sniffed miserably and studied the door desperately. There had to be something there that would help her here.

'Beware of limbo dancers' with an arrow pointing at the bottom of the door.

I.C.A.Q.A.Q.I.C.I.8.2.Q.B.4.I.P

Neither of those gave her any idea what she should do next nor did the scribbled Sylvia Plath poem that curled around the lock.

Then she saw something written in faded pink along the edge of the door. She couldn't quite make it out. Standing up she pulled her knickers up, tugged her skirt down and crouched down in front of the door.

One finger touched the first letter and ran along the sentence. She read it aloud. 'Life is short, start with dessert.'

Jilly bit her lower lip, scraping off a layer of Plush Pink lipstick, and stood up. Head held high, she pushed open the door of the stall and walked out of the toilets, out of the Empire altogether, in search of dessert.